FIFTY SHADES OF SNOW

PART 3

A. ROY MILLIGAN

ISBN: 9798359855402

CHAPTER **ONE**

The guy who had been driving the Suburban got out, pissed off, until he saw Steve slumped over the steering wheel. Smoke was pouring out of the front end, the windshield was shattered, and what was left of the front of the car was completely flattened. Steve showed no signs of consciousness. The man's heart went from racing due to anger, to racing due to panic. The situation did not look good at all.

"Hey, man!" the guy yelled out. "Hey!" He pulled on the driver's side door, but it was locked. He walked around the car to try and see if there was a place he could get in at. Another white guy, who looked to be about 50 years old, pulled over and walked up to the scene.

"I called the police. They should be here soon," he said calmly while surveying the scene.

"Help me get this guy out," the driver of the Suburban said, still trying to find a way into the car.

"You don't think we should wait until the police arrive?"

"Not with all this smoke. This could turn into a fire and explode."

"You know this guy or something?"

He looked up from the passenger side of the car with a look of rage on his face. "Get the hell out of here!" he yelled, noticing that the other guy didn't plan to be of any use. He wondered if he wasn't doing anything because Steve was black.

"Fuck you, man!" the other gentleman yelled back, giving him the finger. He got in his car and sped off.

The guy shook his head as he saw him drive away, then yelled out again, "Hey! Are you okay? Can you hear me?"

By now, the scene was swarming with people. Some had their phones out recording the action while some just stood there watching, not knowing exactly what to do. The guy had checked all the doors, and they were locked. The police were still nowhere in sight. He walked up to the passenger door, and kicked the window. Nothing. He kicked it again, and it shattered. He knocked some of the glass out with his elbow, reached in, and unlocked the door. He got into the passenger seat, and checked Steve's pulse.

He slapped him gently on his cheek and yelled, "Hey, man. Wake up!" Steve woke up, but was confused. All he could see were airbags, blood, and some guy he didn't know. He didn't really quite remember that he had been in an accident. "Shit, what the fuck?"

"Hey, I'm here to help you. You just got in an accident. You need to get out of the car. I'll help you." He hit the power lock on the passenger door, unlocking all the doors to the car. "I'm going to go around to your door, and help you get out. Hang on a sec," he said as he ran around to the other side of the car.

He pulled on the door. It opened with some effort, but stopped about halfway due to all the front end damage.

"The seat belt won't unbuckle," Steve said, fiddling with his buckle with no success. Steve tried to pull slack out in the belt, but it was locked up. The guy reached over him and tried to pull the belt himself. Nope, it was jammed.

"Fire!" one of the onlookers yelled out. There was an engine fire starting in what was left of the front end. Steve could feel his feet and legs getting warm, almost like the flames were underneath the car as well.

"Oh, shit!" Steve yelled as he saw the flames engulf the front end of the car.

The guy reached around to his hip, removing a pocket knife he had clipped to his belt. He opened it up and handed it to Steve. Steve started cutting the seatbelt while the guy pulled it apart with his hands, keeping the belt tight so the knife would cut through it better.

"It's on fire! Get out of there!" a lady yelled as she recorded the scene.

"Oh, my God," another lady said as she covered her mouth.

"That's it. You're almost there," the guy encouraged him. Steve cut through the belt, and the guy reached out and took his hand. Steve gripped his hand and tried to get his legs out of the door. His left leg moved, but his right leg was stuck under the dash. Steve started to panic.

"Relax. I got you. Stay calm. Stay calm."

"I can't get my leg out. It's stuck," Steve said as he looked at him with a face filled with desperation. The guy bent down, climbing into the driver's side leg space to try and see if he could free Steve's leg. It wouldn't move. It was hot in there, and the flames started coming out from the bottom of the car. The guy got his hands around Steve's shoe, which was soaked in blood along with his whole right leg, and pulled. His leg came free, and the guy fell backwards out of the car. He then scrambled back to his feet to help Steve. Steve wrapped his arm around the guy's neck, and he helped him away from the car. The flames made their way back in the car, and within 30 seconds, the whole car was burning. He set Steve down on the ground, and started checking him over to see where the bleeding was coming from. A woman ran up with an emergency first aid kit in her hand. Sirens could be heard coming in the distance, but they didn't sound like they were close.

CHAPTER **TWO**

The woman pulled out some gauze, and put it onto a cut in Steve's leg, applying direct pressure in an attempt to stop the bleeding. The driver of the Suburban sat down next to Steve to catch his breath.

Steve was in severe pain. His whole body hurt, and he didn't even think about what might be broken or bleeding. He was just happy to be away from that car. Steve turned his head and looked at the guy next to him and smiled.

"Thanks, man. I appreciate this. You saved my life," Steve said as he went to place his hand on the guy's back, but a sharp pain shot through his left shoulder and Steve winced in pain.

"Just relax. It's no problem at all," he responded, putting his arm around Steve and giving him a hug. "Oh yeah," he continued, reaching his hand in his pocket. "I got this for you. Figured you might want it," he said, handing him his cell phone.

Steve smiled and nodded. "Damn, thank you. Yes, I need this for sure." Steve reached into his right pocket to check for his other phone. *Thank God! It's still there,* he thought as he felt it in his pocket. Steve sent a quick text to James, telling him that he had been in an accident and that his car was totaled. He asked him if he could come get him.

They were surrounded by people and cars. Everyone swarmed them now, asking if they were okay and what had happened. The lady with the first aid kit just sat there, diligently holding the gauze to his leg. Steve still couldn't remember much about what had happened. He had hit his head pretty hard, and was still shaken up.

The police were the first to arrive on the scene. One officer started telling people to clear the area, and squatted down next to Steve.

"Is everyone okay?" the officer asked.

"He's bleeding from the leg," the woman responded, "but it's slowed down significantly."

"You two weren't in the accident?" the officer asked.

"I wasn't. I just came here to help," she responded.

"We were," Steve and the Suburban driver replied in unison.

The officer continued to ask them questions, and decided to give Steve a breathalyzer, which he passed. The ambulance arrived just as the officer was finishing the test. Steve bit his tongue in the car crash, and his leg was bleeding. The paramedics checked him over, cleaned up the wound on his leg, and wrapped it up for him. Steve didn't feel the need to go to the hospital to get checked for anything else.

James was almost there, since he dropped everything he was doing to come to check on Steve. He made a call to his mom, telling her to call his insurance company to make a claim on the car, or what was left of it. Steve thanked the guy in the Suburban again, and they exchanged numbers. Steve said he wanted to keep in touch since he had saved his life. A couple minutes later, James arrived.

"That's your car?" he asked, pointing to the tow truck which had the remnants of his vehicle loaded up on it.

"Yeah, that's it."

"Damn, you good though?"

"I'm alright, just fucked my leg up a little, but I don't need stitches or anything, so I'm straight. I'm ready to get the hell outta here."

"Say less," James replied, opening his passenger door, and helping Steve get in.

CHAPTER **THREE**

James drove away from the scene and looked over at his friend, who still seemed to be in a daze.

"Damn, what happened?"

Steve shook his head. "Shit, I just escaped death. I was looking down at a text message and slammed into the back of somebody. Almost got fucked up bad, but I'm straight. Just got a couple scrapes. That's all."

"You tripping. You about to kill yourself over a text?"

"Man, I'm done with this bitch. My uncle was right the whole time. She was dragging me down for sure. I shoulda listened to you a LONG time ago, man. I was looking at a sex video of this bitch when I hit that Suburban. I looked up, and all the traffic was stopped dead. I was doing like 55 mph when I looked up and saw that shit stopped like 5 feet in front of me. I'ma kill this bitch."

"What you talking about? A sex video?"

"Yeah, a video of her giving a nigga head." Steve balled up his fist. He wanted to punch something. He couldn't wait to see Angelia.

"Yeah, you gotta be done with her, bro. I keep listening to you and trying to be supportive when you say you gone work stuff out with her. I tried and tried to be on your side, but this is getting ridiculous. You gotta be done with her, bro."

"Done with her? I'm killing this hoe when I get home. I'm not even going to say shit. I'ma just choke her until she stops breathing. Like, fuck you, bitch!" he yelled as he put his hands up like he was choking her out.

"Damn, chill out, bro. She's not even worth all that. Just leave her alone. Why is it so hard for you to leave her alone? Y'all got herpes or something together? This shit starting to get weird . . . or you just a whole sucka and a half. I'm not sure anymore."

"This is it. For real, I ain't playing. Look at this shit," Steve said as he showed him a video on his phone. James watched the video, shaking his head. Angelia looked like a professional porn star in the video.

"Who is the dude?"

"I don't know," Steve said, swiping through the video, getting to the part where he could see the dude fucking Angelia.

"Yeah, I don't know him neither. Damn, Shila sent you this shit?"

"Hell yeah, and she said she has more. I'm like, this shit crazy. I'm tired of going through this shit. This bitch got all these skeletons in her closet. Now she pregnant."

"She pregnant?" James asked, glancing at Steve with big eyes as the light turned green and he started driving again.

"Yeah, man." Steve shook his head.

"Abortion. Fuck that."

"She ain't gone get no damn abortion."

"Even if you pay her, she won't?"

"I don't know. I mean, I don't want to kill my only child either." Steve stared down at the floor of the passenger seat. James could tell he was thinking about everything. It wasn't about Angelia. Steve was the soft one and James understood that for sure.

"I feel you. So what you gone do?"

"I don't know. I need help. What would you do . . . FUCK!!!" Steve screamed out of nowhere.

James looked over at him. "What the fuck?"

"My money! My money burned the fuck up in the car crash."

CHAPTER **FOUR**

"Oh, shit! How much?"

"Three hundred thousand. Damn, let me call the broker. I had an appointment at three o'clock with him to get the hotel." Steve called John and explained everything to him about the accident. John was very understanding and told him that they could just meet tomorrow. John believed Steve and knew that he wasn't trying to play any games with him.

James didn't want to take Steve straight home. He wanted to give him some time to chill and think. James drove to his house, and they sat in the living room. Steve's head was starting to clear up a little bit, and although he was still sore all over, he was feeling much better overall. They went through the details of how Steve should handle Angelia. James tried to help him construct a plan that made sense, and wouldn't cause any issues. Steve insisted on beating her ass, but after a few minutes, James talked him out of it. James reminded him that she was pregnant, and it could hurt the baby. He encouraged Steve to go get his drugs and money out of the house before he made any other moves. Steve was listening, but he was burning with rage inside. It took everything inside of him not to head straight there and call her out.

"I'm not sure if I can hold my composure around her when I see her. She hurt me bad, bro. Like I'm really sick. I'm so sick, I'm calm." Steve thought for a minute and looked up at James and said, "She not gone play with my money though, bro."

"You tripping. You don't know what she gone do. She's proven that. Y'all engaged and she just found out she's pregnant, and now you want to leave? She's going to kill you, bro," James said with a serious look on his face.

"Hell naw. It's all her fault. What she gone kill me for? It's her fault, not mine."

"I feel you. I just don't think it's gone play out good for you."

"I know my girl, bro. She's going to be mad, but she will be okay."

"Do you really? You say you know her, but she keep showing you how she is. You know what . . . If you say so. Sure, everything gone be okay. So, you gone call Shila back and see what else she got for you?"

"Yeah. I already set up a time to meet with her later. I'ma just trick Angelia out the house and go get my shit when she leaves."

"That will work. Send her shopping. You know she won't turn that shit down."

They both started laughing for the first time today. "She might be gone now. When I left earlier, Candy had just came over there. Let me text her." Steve pulled out his phone.

CHAPTER **FIVE**

Steve: Wyd?

Angelia: Came to the mall with Candy.

Steve: Oh okay.

Angelia: What's up? You miss me?

That pissed Steve off. "This bitch just asked me if I miss her."

"Keep calm. You can go off later. Just say you miss her."

Steve: Yeah, I miss you.

Angelia: I miss you too, Papi. We going to celebrate later on. I'm grabbing more liquor and some snacks and stuff that way we don't have to leave out for anything. We can just enjoy each other.

Steve: Sounds good to me. See you later.

Angelia: I love you.

"I'm not saying I love you back. Fuck that!"

"You got to. What you mean?" James said, laughing. "You got all that shit and money in that house. If you want to get it out of there safely, keep shit cool. We will be there in 20 minutes."

Steve: I love you too.

"Where you going to take all this shit to? Have you even thought about that yet?"

"Damn, I haven't. I don't know. FUCK!"

"How much is it?"

"A lot. A whole lot."

"Damn."

"Let's just wait. I'ma go see what Shila has to tell me then I will go from there. I gotta chill out and think."

"You bet not take Angelia back, bro. That ain't cool."

"I'm not this time. I'm done for real. I've lost my plug over her and everything."

"What? You lost the plug?" James asked, confused.

"Yeah, Swift talking about, leave her alone or he cutting me off because she going to get me killed or arrested. So he cut me off. I have to pay the plug, then I guess that's it."

"That's not good. Not good at all, man. I was just talking to Juice, and he was saying he wanted you to meet these New York dudes he be fucking with that be grabbing some major weight."

Steve shook his head. Angelia had caused a lot of problems for him. He could feel his anger rising again, then he calmed himself down and replied, "Maybe I can get it back once Swift sees that I'm done with her for good."

"I woulda chose the plug over her. You really tripping. You can get a chick like her anywhere. You can't just get a plug like that overnight. That's a street niggas dream. You got that shit handed to you and you just gone give it up for a chick that don't even respect you? A chick that you caught fucking another dude in your own place, then she acts like she ain't did shit wrong? A chick that you got ON VIDEO with another ni-."

Steve cut him off. "I know. I get it, bro. Trust me, I get it. I was just thinking that she really loved me like I loved her. I mean, people make mistakes."

"See, there you go again making excuses. Look, bro, she maybe do love you even more than you love her, but that don't mean you have to deal with whatever she throws your way. She shoulda been cut off." James shook his head.

CHAPTER
SIX

Steve picked up his phone and called back the number Shila called him on.

"Hello."

"Where do you want to meet up at?" he asked.

"Meet me at my house. I'm making dinner. I have food on right now."

"Okay. Your kids there?"

"No, why?"

"Just asking. I didn't want to interrupt."

"You good. You can come by now."

"Okay. I'm heading over there now then."

"See you soon," Shila said, hanging up.

James turned around and started heading to Shila's house once Steve told him where she lived. They weren't too far away from her house, so it only took 7 minutes to get to her subdivision. Steve noticed the look on James' face when they got close.

"Damn, these houses are nice as hell. Me and my wife gone move into something nice like this in the next few years," James commented.

"Yeah, these are nice as hell for sure. You should see the inside of Shila's place. She got the decorating on point, nice and clean."

James continued to drive until he got toward the back of the subdivision, and finally pulled into Shila's driveway. He gave Steve a pound. He told him to hit him up if he needed a ride later. Steve got out and walked up to the front door. He realized this was his first time coming through the front door, or even paying attention to it. In the past, he always pulled into her garage and went in. The front door was a large, polished wooden double door with side lights. Steve knocked and heard Shila yell out from inside, "Who is it?"

"Steve."

"Why didn't you call me?" she said as she opened up the door. "You coulda pulled in the garage."

"I didn't drive. I got dropped off. I was in a car accident."

"Oh, my God," Shila said, hugging him as she closed the door behind him. "Are you okay?"

"Yeah, I'm good. I got a little cut on my leg, but nothing major. The car is totaled though. That muthafucka burned all the way to the springs." Steve thought about telling her that the video she sent to him was the reason he slammed into the back of the truck and almost killed himself. He decided not to bring it up.

CHAPTER **SEVEN**

Shila's mouth dropped. "I seen that on the news. They got the whole video. I didn't know that was you. A white guy pulled you out the car, right?"

"Yup."

"Wow, I was just talking to my girl about that. That was a nice car you had too."

"Yeah, that guy saved me for sure, and I did like that car. My foot was stuck, and my seatbelt was jammed up. I'm glad that dude was there."

"You are blessed. Oh, my God. I can't believe that was you. You was in the car by yourself? That was right after we texted."

"I was by myself. Yes, right after."

"What happened?"

"I was reaching for some shit and wasn't paying attention."

"You better keep your eyes on the road from now on," she replied, giving him a light punch in the arm. Steve grabbed at his shoulder. Shila put her arm out, looking concerned. "Did I just hurt you?"

"No, you good. My left shoulder just got bruised up a little bit by the seatbelt. I'm just kinda sore all over. But yeah, I'ma keep my eyes on the road for sure going forward. That shit shook my ass up!" he said, laughing.

Steve noticed that something smelled incredible when he walked in the door, but wanted to get the accident discussion out of the way before he said anything. "It smells good as hell in here. What you cooking?"

Shila laughed. "Filet mignon steaks in the sous vide with some garlic mashed potatoes and gravy. I made some greens too. I love greens."

"Yeah, me too. That all sounds perfect." Shila looked great to Steve. She was wearing some butt shorts, but she had light pink, silk sleepwear on top.

"So, you got caught dealing with me, I see?"

"Y . . . yeah, and I didn't mean any of that shit I said to you. Angelia was tripping out on me. I thought she was gone stab me or something."

She giggled. "I wasn't offended. I knew she made you say some stuff for sure."

"What's up with you and Angelia anyway?" Steve asked. "You ain't spinning me this time. I want to know what's what. It's like you been had a vendetta against her."

"Follow me. I'll tell you all about it."

CHAPTER **EIGHT**

Shila walked him into the living room where she had her camera already hooked up to her TV. She turned the TV on, and Angelia was on the TV on all fours with the guy behind her. She pressed play, and Steve watched. She was getting fucked all kinds of different ways. Steve didn't even want to watch anymore, so he looked away. His heart fell in his stomach, and he swallowed hard. Shila could tell he was hurt so she turned off the TV, and told Steve to come into the kitchen. Steve sat down at the kitchen table, and put his head in his hands.

"Why you ain't send me that video too?" he asked.

"Because I wanted to see you," she said, giving him a wink and a smile.

Steve took a deep breath and cleared his throat. "You got more videos than that one you just showed me?"

Shila gave him a slow and serious nod. "Yes, a lot more to be honest. I'ma send them to you so you can go ahead and get rid of her. She ain't shit."

"Do you know the dude in the video?"

Shila stared at him, put her hands on the island, leaned forward, and took a deep breath. "Yeah, that's my baby daddy."

"Wow! So that's why you don't like her. I get it now. I just thought you hated her ass because I was with her."

"Exactly. I just didn't want to start shit. Believe it or not, I wanted you, but I wanted to keep the peace."

"So how long she been dealing with your baby daddy?" Steve asked, still in shock at the information.

"She been dealing with Ace for like 5 years. She the reason me and him fell out so many times with each other."

"5 years? Damn, so she been playing me forever. This shit is crazy. So these videos go back that far?"

"Yup."

"Why did he give them to you?"

"Oh, he didn't give them to me. I stole them."

Steve shook his head and slid back in his chair. He felt so stupid. His heart rate started increasing and he could feel the extreme anger coming back to the surface. He took a few deep breaths, trying to calm himself down. "Good looking. Excuse me for a second. I gotta send a quick message."

"Oh, no problem. Do whatever you need to do," she said as she stirred the potatoes on the stove. Steve sent James a text message telling him to come back and get him. He was trying not to freak out, trying not to let the tears fall from his eyes. Shila saw the pain in his face and could hear it in his voice. She walked over to him, and stood behind him, resting her hands on both of his shoulders. "I know you hurt. I want you to know that my intentions were never to hurt your feelings." She started massaging his shoulders gently. "I think it's sexy that you actually have feelings and can show them in front of me. Most guys try to suppress them and act like everything is alright, even when it's not. I'm okay if you have to vent, cry, pout, complain, or whatever you need to do to ease the pain. I'm here for you and I want you to know that you can stay here as long as you need to, if you need to, until you get your situation all figured out. I'm sorry that it didn't work out with you and her, but you deserve much better than that. I woulda never ever played you like that. She's been playing with you the whole time. Like I said, you deserve better, and I'm hoping that you are starting to see what you're truly worth."

CHAPTER
NINE

Tears fell from his eyes as she continued to talk. She kept rubbing his shoulders as she attempted to console him with her words the best she knew how. Her shoulder rubbing felt good on his sore body. She was doing it just right, not too hard, not too soft. He could feel some of the stress and tension of the day leaving him, though he was still insanely mad about what Angelia had been doing to him all this time. He picked up his phone, and texted James telling him never mind about coming to get him. He made up his mind that he was just going to stay put for now. He was scared that if he went home, he might do something stupid. His phone started to ring. It was James.

"You mind if I step out to take this call?"

"It's a room in the back on the left. Go in there for as long as you want. It's just a guest room, so you can make yourself at home."

Steve thanked her, and picked up his phone on the way to the room. He closed the door, and sat down on the bed.

"What's up?"

"You good?"

Steve laughed. "Yeah, I was about to leave then I changed my mind. I'ma just chill here for a lil' bit, but I think I want you to go grab all my stuff out of there."

"That's probably a good idea. I'll go get it for you and bring it to you if you want."

"All I want is my money and you know what. You going to need my truck. The keys to it is on my dresser. You know where everything else is."

"Okay, bro. I'll go get it right now before she gets back. Me and Eboni are both going to go so she can follow behind me."

"Thanks, bro. I appreciate this a whole lot. You really helping me out on this one."

"You want me to set up the video to play for her when she walks in the house?" James asked.

Steve laughed knowing James was good with all the techy stuff. "Yeah, I don't care. I'll send them to you. Let me know once you leave. I'll send her a piece of my mind. She gone lose her shit."

"Okay, I got you. We about to head over there right now. I'll hit you in a little while."

"Bet." Steve hung up the phone feeling a little better. He knew that he needed to get away from Angelia. There was no way around it. This was it. He was completely destroyed inside. It was all in his face and he couldn't hide it.

When he came back into the kitchen, she had a short glass of dark liquor waiting for him on the island. He smiled, then downed the whole thing, hoping that it would take some of the pain away. He didn't have an appetite, although what she was cooking looked and smelled delicious.

She had steaks in a sous vide, and all she needed to do was sear them quickly on each side and they'd be done. She was waiting until he was off the phone so they would be perfect for him. She poured Steve another drink then she seared the steaks, and made him a plate. He sat down and took a few sips of his drink. Although he wasn't hungry, once he took a bite, everything was so good, he finished every last bite off the plate.

CHAPTER **TEN**

It took James some time to get everything into the truck, but it all worked out. James brought everything to him knowing if he would have gotten pulled over, he would have never seen his family ever again, except for in the visiting room of a prison. He would have been doing life with the amount of cash and cocaine he had on him. Steve hated putting him in that position, but he thought back to what his uncle told him about. He had to get this done. When dealing with this much weight, there was no room for error.

James brought Steve's truck to Shila's house, and parked it in the garage with all his stuff in it. It was fine for now, but he'd need to move it soon. Steve instructed James to take a duffle bag with him that had $500,000 in it. He kept his money very neat, in blocks which made it easy to count. James brought $100,000 to Steve's mom, and put the rest in a storage unit. Steve needed some time to clear his head.

Shila gathered all the videos she had, and gave them to Steve. She told him that he should consider her place his place for as long as he needed. She assured him that her kids would be gone for at least a few days. She fully understood what he was going through, because Ace had done the same thing to her, over and over again.

He brought the bottle of liquor in the guest room with him and laid down on the bed. The bed faced a nice 60" curve TV that was mounted on the wall, and Steve turned on the videos Shila gave him. He started crying almost from the start of the videos. It was Angelia for sure, but it was hard for him to believe it. It was one thing to know that she had cheated, and another thing to catch a guy pounding her from behind. But this was totally different seeing hours of footage of her in action with another man.

Steve cried out to God, asking what he did to deserve all the pain he was feeling. He tipped back the bottle, taking a few big gulps, hoping that it would numb the pain. For some reason, it didn't seem to be working, so he drank more. The more he watched, the worse his pain got. His thoughts raced as he watched the scenes in front of him. He began pondering all the good times they had over the years, and wondered if everything was just a big joke to her the whole time. It seemed to him that she loved him over the years, but watching this made him question everything. He got up from the bed as a new video started. He took a few more swigs off the bottle as he stood in front of the TV. The date on the video was in the same week as his birthday. He thought back to what they did together that week, and it cut him so deep he fell to his knees in tears. He pounded the floor, and cursed the fact that he had ever met her. All she had done was cause him immense pain and heartache.

Steve felt like he had completely lost control of his emotions. The anger, pain, fear, anxiety, hurt, and disappointment were overwhelming him. He got up from the floor, and sat on the end of the bed, wiping his eyes and taking another drink. He couldn't believe she had played him this bad. The guy was being rough with her, and not using condoms while he came inside her again and again. Steve wondered how big of an idiot he must've been over the years to not notice that something was going on. He would never have guessed that she was cheating on him until the one time he caught her. He especially thought that she would never cheat on him while being recorded like this.

CHAPTER ELEVEN

He watched her suck Ace's dick like it was the love of her life. Steve shook his head and took a few more big drinks from his bottle. He watched Ace pound Angelia in her ass, which was something he never thought she'd like as much as what the videos were showing. He watched Ace cum across her face, and cum in her mouth and she swallowed. He couldn't even count the number of times he saw Ace dump his load inside her pussy. It was disgusting to him. He got up and paced again, drinking from the bottle and staring at the TV. The alcohol started to take effect, but it wasn't calming him down, that's for sure. He felt like dying. He found himself standing in the corner, and he slid himself down the wall until he sat on the hardwood floor. He was holding his bottle and shaking and sniffling. This was the worst pain he had ever felt. His body felt empty, except for what felt like razorblades in his stomach, that felt like they cut deeper every time he moved. He started to feel lightheaded, almost like he was going to pass out. He wanted to yell out and scream, but he kept silently crying, not wanting Shila to hear him. Despite all the other challenges and heartaches in his life, this was hurting him the worst. He blew his nose again and again, but it kept refilling with snot and running down on his lip as he sobbed.

He stood up and looked at himself in the mirror on the back of the bedroom door. He shook his head. He looked pathetic and felt humiliated. Tears ran down his face, and his eyes were red and puffy.

It was as if every single person knew that Angelia had been cheating on him except for him. He couldn't bring himself to understand why she would do this to him. Every few minutes, he looked up at the ceiling, crying out silently and hoping to get an answer from God as to why this was happening to him. He quietly whispered to the ceiling, praying for an answer. Steve pounded his fist on the bed. God wasn't responding, so he thought it would be better to just go back to drinking and watching the videos while basking in the pain. Each video was about 30 minutes long, so this went on for hours. Sometimes Ace would be holding the camera while he fucked her. Other times he would have the camera in her face while fucking her in different positions.

Thinking about how she would come home to him after this went on absolutely destroyed Steve. She would come home and lay down next to him, or they would even have sex after she was out being abused by another man. As horrible as watching these videos was, they taught Steve a lot about Angelia, who she was, and what she wanted. There were scenes where they were acting out a rape. Angelia would resist, and Ace would slap her across the face, ball up his fist, and tell her not to move while she curled up on the bed like she was scared. He heard of people having 'pretend rape' sex before, but he had no clue that this was the kind of thing that Angelia enjoyed. Looking at the way Ace treated her sexually made him realize that he obviously hadn't been doing it for her in the bedroom, not even close.

In addition to the sex scenes, Steve came across additional videos of Angelia. Ace had videos of her in exotic cars that he had rented.

Watching her smile, and listening to her voice made him hurt even more. He had videos of her in a bar that he used to own. Some of the footage almost made it seem like they were a couple. It creeped Steve out, but it pissed him off even more. The number of videos that he had of her made Steve understand that Angelia's trust in Ace must have been extremely deep.

As the alcohol pumped through his veins, he thought about all the terrible things he wanted to do to Angelia. He wanted revenge. This wasn't just a break up and walk away situation. He thought about killing her, then he thought about killing himself. His mind wouldn't calm down. He walked around pacing and drinking, while his mind continuing to alternate between hurting her and hurting himself. He made it back to the bed and laid down with his bottle next to him, opening it and taking sips every few minutes while the TV showed the videos. Eventually, he started nodding in and out until he fell asleep.

CHAPTER **TWELVE**

Angelia had been running around all day shopping with Candy. She wanted to buy things for the baby, but figured it was way too early. She did buy Steve a few things. She had been wanting him to dress a little better, so they picked him out some new designer fits. She was having the salesman try on some of the outfits so she could see how they would look on a real person. Candy laughed as Angelia made the guy model for them.

Later, they stopped to eat lunch at one of their favorite restaurants, and talked all about how life would be changing with a new baby. It was a typical girls' day, and they had a blast. Candy drove back to the house while singing loudly in the driver's seat vibing the whole way.

"Girl, you silly as hell. You ain't never gone grow up!" Angelia said, laughing as Candy parked in the driveway. Angelia noticed that the whole house was dark, and Steve's truck was gone.

"You know you love how I do," Candy said with a smile.

"Hey, help me with these bags, girl. You just be trying to drop a bitch off and go!"

Candy giggled. "Whatever, girl. I'll help yo' pregnant ass."

They grabbed all the bags out of the trunk and walked inside through the garage door. Both of their jaws dropped, along with the bags, as they got into the kitchen. They could see all the way to the big screen TV, which was playing a video of her and Ace having sex.

Angelia put her hands over her mouth and wanted to cry. "Oh . . . my . . . God," Candy whispered in a state of shock.

"How the fuck he get this?" Angelia said as she walked through the house turning on all the lights. "Steve!" she shouted, but nobody answered. "Steve!" she yelled out one final time. Silence, except for the sounds of her moans coming from the TV. Angelia ran over to the TV and turned off the power. Candy walked around looking for Steve, but he clearly wasn't home.

"He not here, girl. What's going on? Is that you and Ace?"

"Yes!" Angelia screamed. "I'm trying to figure out how the fuck he got this video. I swear to God, if that bitch gave him this video, I'm going to jail for murder. She trying to ruin my life." Angelia was in full on panic mode. She was pacing around the island, shaking violently with her phone in her hands. She called Steve. He didn't answer. She called again and again, leaving a voicemail each time. She texted him repeatedly, telling him to call her ASAP. Her stomach was in knots. Candy didn't know what to say, so she just stood by to be there for her friend if she needed her. "He's not answering!" Angelia screamed, lifting her phone over her head like she was about to throw it. She then set her phone down on the island and called Ace on speaker. She paced back and forth while it rang three times before he picked up.

CHAPTER **THIRTEEN**

"Hello."

"What the fuck is going on, Ace?" she screamed at the top of her lungs.

"What you mean? Calm down. What's good with you, ma?"

"Don't ma me! How the fuck did Steve get our sex video?"

Ace was speechless. He ran into his closet and pulled out his shoebox where he kept his SD cards of sex videos. He started going through the box.

"What the fuck are you doing? Answer me!" she yelled.

"Hold on. What the fuck is you talking about?"

"Steve had a video playing of us when I just walked into my house! You know what the fuck I'm talking about!"

"I don't. I swear. Hold on, just a second," he said as he looked at the last few cards, but every one with 'Ang' on it was missing.

"How? How, Ace?" she said, as tears started to fall and the reality of the situation became clear to her.

"I didn't let her. Shila had to have stolen them, I'm telling you."

"I thought you said you don't fuck with her anymore. How would she have stole them, Ace, huh?" Angelia's panic and desperation transitioned to anger.

"Let me figure this out. Calm down. I'ma call you back."

She hung up the phone and slammed her hands on the countertop. "I'm going to kill this bitch. It's that simple. She's trying to ruin my life, so I'ma just take hers. If she put these videos on the internet . . . I swear to God, Candy!"

Candy shook her head. She felt for Angelia, but tried to remain calm herself and not make the situation worse. "Yeah, she tripping. Why would she do that? Thirsty ass bitch. I hate thirsty ass bitches." She walked over to Angelia who was pacing again, and put her hand on her shoulder, then pulled her in for a hug.

"I appreciate it," Angelia said, pushing her away gently. "I'm just too mad for a hug right now. That bitch want to be me so bad! She wants everything I got and she be wanting all the dudes I fuck with. I hate this bitch, and now Steve's dumbass not answering the phone," she said as she went back to calling him repeatedly.

"You not lying. I been saying she wanted to be you," Candy said, shrugging her shoulders, still agreeing with Angelia, but trying to keep from working her up too much.

Steve didn't answer, but soon, Ace called back.

CHAPTER
FOURTEEN

"Hello. What did that bitch say?"

"She acted like she didn't know what I was talking about. I know she had to have taken them though for sure. I just told her them videos bet not get out no further than where they at now. So if those videos hit the internet, it's gone be because of your boy, not her. She knows I'm not playing with her ass."

Angelia started crying again, and the tone of her voice changed. "You promised I could trust you and that no one would ever see our videos. I trusted you, Ace. Now look, my life is being ruined over it. I hate that bitch so much. I wish she was dead. I still can't believe you let this happen, Ace."

"I'm sorry. I thought I had them in a safe place," Ace replied again in a calm voice, but Angelia had already hung up the phone.

Angelia walked into the living room and threw herself onto the couch. "Oh, my God, Candy. This is crazy!"

"Well, how many videos is it? And how far back do they go?"

"Hey, try to call Steve's phone from yours, and I don't know how many videos there is. Maybe 7 or 8. Most of them was old, but a few is more recent. We wasn't even fucking like that though. We'd get together maybe 5 times a year, and maybe make one video out of those times. I don't know, but it wasn't that much." Angelia was distracted by listening to the ringing on Candy's phone. She hoped that Steve would pick up.

Candy shook her head after the fourth ring. "Damn, you really going to have to fight for this one, girl. You going to have to give it everything you got. This one is bad. I mean, last time when he caught you and Jon Jon in the bed, you came back from that. To me, that was the worst. You just gotta fight. Give it all you got."

"I'll tell you what I'ma give all I got . . . killing that bitch. I'ma kill her and that's that."

Candy laughed. "You is crazy."

"This bitch is really trying to ruin my life, so I'ma ruin her life back. That's what's fair. It's over for her ass. Steve bet not be with her right now," she said as she scrolled through her phone to find James' number. When she found his contact, she dialed his line.

CHAPTER
FIFTEEN

"Hello."

"Where's Steve?" she asked with an attitude.

"Look, I don't know what y'all got going on, but you don't need to be rude when you call my phone. You can speak."

Angelia took a deep breath then continued in a pleasant voice. "Hi, James. Do you know where my husband is?" she asked with as little sarcasm as possible.

"He at a hotel, chilling. He safe. He probably asleep for real. He was drinking and stressing out bad. Why you keep stressing my nigga out like that?" James had a lot more he wanted to say to her, but he kept it at that.

"He stressing his self out. It's not me. All the stuff he been finding out is old. He tripping over old stuff."

"Old don't make him not be hurt about it. You are who he wants to marry, but you making it so hard having recent videos of you fucking other dudes and getting caught with a dude in y'all house," James replied calmly in a low voice.

"First of all, it was one dude on the video. Second of all, he just left and is not answering his phone. I want to talk to him and explain my side of the story. How ever he got those videos is obviously because someone don't like me. This is all intentional, trying to cause problems with us. I need to talk to him face to face. Can you please tell him to call me?"

"I will, but I don't know if he gone listen to me."

"Just try. Do you know what hotel he's at?"

James laughed. "No, I'm not telling you that so you can go stalking and bothering him. It's a good idea to give him some space so he can calm down. He's real upset over this thing, Ang."

"Please, James. You know I love him and want to be with him."

He wanted to say that he couldn't tell based on what he saw in the videos, but he didn't want to make it awkward between them. "I'm not going to tell you. I promised him that I wouldn't, so I'm sticking to that."

"Is he coming back? Why is all his money and stuff gone?" Her voice started to betray her feelings of panic. "James? He knows I can't afford this house! Where is he?" Tears flowed from her eyes as she broke down again. "Please tell him to come back. Please, James. I love him so much. I want to be with him. I'm pregnant, James. Where is he?" She cried more and more, unable to keep speaking. James waited a minute while she tried to get herself together.

"Ang, he didn't tell me exactly what he doing. I know he needs some time, but I promise I'll tell him you want to talk to him. Okay?"

She was still sobbing and crying uncontrollably, but managed to say, "Okay, bye," before hanging up.

When she hung up, she laid down on the floor and cried. Candy got down on the floor next to her in an attempt to cheer her up. "It's only 8 o'clock. He may call in a little bit."

"I want him to call right now," she said, taking her phone out and calling him again.

"It's gone be okay. You need me to do anything? I have to get my boo. I was supposed to get him at 7:30."

"I'm good. Thank you. I'm just about to lay down and try to forget about this shit for now."

"If you don't want to stay alone in this big ol' house tonight, you can come stay at my place."

"I'll see if he come home by midnight, then I'll let you know. I'm about to call Esha over."

"Okay, cool, cheer up. He ain't going nowhere. He just mad right now. He will be back. He ain't gone leave all that sexiness for the next man to get." They both laughed together.

CHAPTER SIXTEEN

Shila was taking a short nap after she ate to try and give Steve some time to be by himself. She was woken up by her phone ringing. It was Ace calling her back to ask about the videos. After she talked to him, she couldn't go back to sleep. She was wondering how Steve was doing downstairs, so she went to check on him. She noticed the door to the garage wasn't shut all the way. She closed it shut and went to the guest room. The door was closed so she gently knocked twice. There was no response, so she knocked again. After a few seconds, she opened the door and peeked inside. The TV was on pause, and he was knocked out, snoring softly with all his clothes on. She walked into the room and examined the liquor bottle that was next to him. It was almost entirely empty, so she knew he had to be pretty drunk. When she had given the bottle to him, it was full. She stood next to the bed, looking down at him, admiring him, and feeling sorry for him at the same time. His phone then started buzzing, and the screen came on saying 'WIFEY' with the number underneath. When she stepped closer to push the button to stop the vibrating, her foot hit something that was sitting part of the way out from under the bed. She looked down and picked up what was clearly a brick of cocaine. The corner of it had been cut, almost as if he had opened it to get some out of there. She held the brick in her hand for a second before noticing a small plate on the nightstand with a hundred dollar bill rolled up next to it.

Her phone started ringing loudly. She jumped and was so startled that she dropped the brick on the floor. Steve opened his eyes at the sound of the phone.

"Heyyy," he said in a half asleep, half drunk voice. He was out of it. When she looked at him, she could tell that he probably wasn't awake enough yet to know where he was.

"Are you okay?" she asked, concerned as he tried to adjust himself in the bed.

"I love you, baby," he slurred while sitting up a little before giving up and falling back on the pillow. He reached out for her. "Lay with me."

"You are drunk, high, or whatever. You acting all weird."

"I'm not. Come here and lay down. I can seeeeee youuuu," he said then closed his eyes for a few seconds before they snapped open again. "I can see you all in my business," he slurred, waving his arm in the direction of the brick on the floor. Shila couldn't help but chuckle a little to herself at his sad condition.

"Who am I? What's my name?" she asked, messing around with him.

"Angeliaaaaaa, my baby," he slurred. Her hand instantly connected with the side of his face, and the smack seemed to reconnect him with reality quickly.

"What the fuck you smack me for, Shila?" he asked as he held his cheek with his hand.

"Oh, you know my name now, huh?" she said, stepping away from the bed and looking down at him with her arms crossed.

"Don't call me by that hoe's name, ever."

Steve struggled, but finally sat himself up in the bed. He remembered where he was and could see who it was standing in front of him. "My bad, I'm fucked up. You know I didn't mean that, my bad."

"I see that. I didn't know you did coke."

"You want some?" he asked, giving her a stupid grin and bending over the side of the bed to pick up the brick she had dropped.

"No, I'm good. I don't do drugs, boo boo."

"Oh, my bad. You mad at me? Don't judge me. I know I'm fucking up right now. I'm trying to get this girl off my mind. I actually just started doing coke not even a week ago." He set the brick next to him on the bed, sat upright, and straightened up his shirt, trying to make himself appear a little bit sober.

CHAPTER SEVENTEEN

Shila shook her head and fought back a smile. She felt so sorry for him. He was so drunk, high, and stressed over Angelia. She admired him for trying to act normal for a minute. She wished a guy would act like this over her. She wished that she could make a man feel the way that Steve felt about Angelia. Clearly, he loved her, and it made Shila a little jealous.

"Can you forgive me? I'll stop once I get over her. I promise."

Shila giggled. "You're fine. Do what you do. I'm not judging you at all. I'm a little surprised to be honest, but not judging at all. Coke is common. A lot of people do it and don't talk about it. You're fine. As long as you don't start smoking crack, we good." She sat down next to him on the bed and he put his arm around her.

Steve laughed. "Hell naw. You never have to worry about that ever. I'm never smoking crack."

"I don't know about that," she joked. "She got you over here a little stressed out I see."

Steve looked down at the floor. "We been together for a long time. She's the only girl I been dealing with for a while, so I'm hurt and shit, but I'll get through it."

"Well, take your time. I know it won't happen overnight. I'm here for you for whatever you need."

"Thanks, and yeah, I know it won't happen overnight. I'ma just take a few days and get fucked up, you know? That's all I want to do."

"Well, you can do that here all you want as long as my kids aren't here and you don't leave anything out."

"For . . . sure. I respect . . . that . . . and . . . and . . . I respect your house. I'll . . . be sober for the kids for sure," he said, swaying as he tried to stay sitting upright.

Shila giggled again as she stood up and looked at his pitiful condition. He was pretty funny when he was drunk and high. "Damn, you had a rough day today. It started with a car accident, and then you found out about your wifey. I'd say you are doing pretty good, but that's pretty messed up." She smiled and pushed him, and he fell back on the bed.

"Wait, how you know that's my wifey?" he asked as he rolled on his side, putting his elbow on the bed and holding his head up with his hand. "You been checking my phone or something?" He started looking around on the bed for his phone. Shila was laughing. When he found it, he had 135 missed calls. 130 of them were from Angelia.

CHAPTER **EIGHTEEN**

"I wouldn't go through your phone. You crazy. I seen it pop up when she was calling. I came in to check on you and see how you were holding up."

"Damn, she won't stop calling."

"Answer it then, and tell her how you feel," she suggested.

"Fuck her. I ain't answering shit," he said, going through all the text messages she had sent.

Angelia's texts:

-Call me.

-Call me ASAP.

-Call me, Papi.

-We need to talk.

-Call me.

-Steve, call me please.

-Papi, please call me. I need to talk to you.

-Are you coming home tonight?

-Call me so I can explain and we can move on with our lives.

-Steve!!! Please call me, please.

-Steve, call me!

-I'm so sorry you had to see that. Let me explain, please.

They went on and on and on. She left so many messages saying the same things, he got tired of reading them. He went to the voicemails, and they all said pretty much the same thing. She wanted to meet with him to talk in person, but Steve wasn't trying to talk.

"You going to have to talk to her eventually," Shila said, leaning back on the wall opposite from Steve. He put his phone down and shook his head.

"I'd rather wait until I get my mind together. Right now, I don't want to be bothered with her. I'll say something stupid or do something stupid if I don't get my head together first."

Shila walked toward him and laid down on the bed, on her side facing him. "You mind being bothered with me?" she asked, smiling with an irresistibly sexy smile.

Steve laughed. "Yeah, that's cool. I don't mind if you bother me."

"You want to come and get in the jacuzzi? I know you had a rough day, and you probably sore from that accident. You need to soak your body in some hot water. It'll feel good, and it will help relax your back and neck muscles. You probably got whiplash from the accident. I know you drunk, but I'll help you get in there." She smiled, stood up, and held out her hand, inviting him to come with her.

He took a deep breath, scooted to the edge of the bed, and took her hand.

"I'll rub your feet, your back, and all that," she said, pulling him to his feet and steadying him with her other hand.

"Okay, I'm down," he said right before losing his footing and falling back onto the bed, taking her with him. "Shit," he said as they both laughed. "I guess I am tipsy."

She laughed again. "I bet you are. You drank pretty much the whole bottle. There was only a little bit left. Let's try this again," she said, getting to her feet and widening her stance dramatically so she could help him up. She pulled him to his feet and caught him once he was standing. She did her best to keep him standing. They walked down the hallway together, and he leaned on her as they made their way out of the room and toward the bottom of the stairs. "Okay, turn right here. Go up the stairs. Be careful, one foot at a time."

CHAPTER **NINETEEN**

He grabbed the handrail with one hand, and held her hand with his other one. "I got this," he said, but he stumbled, dropping to a knee on the bottom step. Shila laughed. Steve didn't have the balance or energy to make it up. "I'ma have to crawl up these bitches. I feel like I'ma fall all the way down."

She giggled. "Steve, you still at the bottom. Okay, you go, and I'll come behind you."

He started crawling up the stairs, and he was pretty successful on his own. Shila was behind him laughing her ass off the whole way up. "I should be recording this right now. You look hilarious." He tried to look back at her to give her a dirty look, but fell into the railing. She laughed even harder.

"Whatever," he said, getting back into his crawling position and making his way up a few more steps. "You bet not record me," he mumbled as he tried to focus on the task at hand. He laughed at himself. "Shit, I'm tired. How many stairs was that?" he asked when he got to the top.

"Oh, my God. You are silly. I don't know how many stairs I have. I've never counted them. One flight. Is that a good answer?"

"Either way, that was a lot of stairs. What time is it?" he asked as he sat and leaned back against the wall to catch his breath.

"It's about 10:30. What time you gotta be home?" she joked with him.

"I don't have a home anymore," he said, as he rose to his feet. He tried pointing at her while his arm waved around. "I gotta find a new home."

She laughed at him again. "You can make this your home if you want to." He put his arm around her shoulder, partly to try and be sweet, and partly for balance.

"Oh, I can?"

"Yup. We would love to have you here."

They crossed the doorway into the bathroom. He balanced himself on the sink and looked at himself in the mirror. "I'ma think about that."

"You should," she said as she got a towel and other things ready for him. "We would be a great team together. And you will love me. I would treat you so good. I know you a good man and I would be honored to have you here every night sleeping next to me." She sat the towel on the edge of the jacuzzi. "I know you going to forget everything I'm saying by the time you wake up tomorrow, so I'ma have to tell you again," she said, giggling.

"No. I'm not going to forget. I can't walk right now, and I'm having a hard time keeping my balance. That's for sure, but I hear you loud and clear. Trust me, I hear you."

"Do you believe what I'm telling you though?"

"I want to. Trust me, I do. The problem is that I'm sure I'm going to have some big time trust issues after this break up."

"It's okay. I understand that. That would be expected after what you've gone through. Come over here and let's get you into the jacuzzi."

He took a couple steps toward her while trying to take off his shirt. He realized that he could barely walk, let alone pull his shirt over his head while walking. "You got the water in there already?"

"No, let me do that first," she said, giggling.

"See, I'm more sober than you. You're the one acting like you been drinking." He sat down at the edge of the tub while the water filled. He pulled out his phone to see what had happened during their journey to the bathroom. Angelia had called four times, sent multiple texts, and left two more voicemails crying and telling him to come home.

CHAPTER
TWENTY

"Okay, by the time we get you undressed and you make it in there, it will be full," Shila said, pulling his shirt over his head.

"Hey, you ain't gone get in with me?" he asked.

Shila smiled. "Of course I am, but we need to get your clothes off. I'm pretty sure you not capable of doing that yourself," she said, giggling to herself. "I'm going to pull your shorts down. Stand up for me." She took his hands and stood him up then pulled his shorts off, lowering them to the floor. He went to take a step like they weren't still around his ankles, and he fell backwards into the jacuzzi full of water. When his head came back up out of the water, he wiped his eyes and took a breath.

"That's one way to get in," she joked with him. "You okay though? I'm coming in right now."

"Yeah, I'm good. I just want you in here with me."

She turned on the jets and the water started to rumble and bubble, then Steve watched her take all her clothes off and climb in. She sat herself down behind him and started to massage his shoulders, neck, and arms. "This feels good, baby. Thank you."

"You welcome. Just relax. I got you on whatever you need or want," Shila whispered into his ear while continuing to rub his neck and shoulders.

Steve let out a soft moan. The massaging hurt just a little bit, but felt great. He could feel his muscles relaxing in the hot water.

"So, did you miss me ever since I blocked you?" he asked, looking back at her to see her response.

"Yes! Oh, my goodness. I missed you so much. I've been so pissed off. I had to take a trip to try and get my mind off you, because I had to respect the fact that you had a girl. That was so hard for me to do."

"You was thinking about me a lot?"

"Yes! All the time. I couldn't stop. I tried to stop when you wasn't answering, but all I could do was think about you."

"What you was thinking about?"

"Just you overall. I really like you and have so much respect for you. I see all the things you do, and I'm impressed. You a good dude. You cool, fun to be around, you keep yourself together, you don't be all in the streets messing with all these hoodrats . . . you have a lot of qualities that I love. I'm thankful every time I get to spend time with you. I was really missing you when you had me blocked."

She kept massaging his shoulders. He felt so relaxed that he almost wanted to just slide forward underneath the water and take a nap. He still felt slightly tense, but his muscles in his neck and back were starting to ease up.

"I missed you too. I appreciate you having me over like this. Not many people are there to help someone when they are at their worst. I don't deal with many people so I woulda been in a hotel room or something by myself just getting fucked up. This is much better for me than that would be. Yeah, I'm fucked up right now, but I'm like a cool fucked up. I feel good. I'm almost feeling a little numb right now."

"That's good," she said, giving him a kiss on his cheek. "I like seeing you happy. I want to always make you happy, and I will do that if you give me the chance."

"We gone see what's up." Steve looked around the tub. "Where my liquor go?"

Shila giggled. "That's almost gone. You drank like the whole bottle. You want me to go get the rest of it? I have another bottle down there I can open for you, but your ass gone mess around and get alcohol poisoning if you're not careful."

"I got this. I won't get alcohol poisoning. Go ahead and get that bottle."

CHAPTER TWENTY-ONE

Shila climbed out of the tub and started to walk out of the door. "And get that plate with the coke on it too," Steve said as she left. She popped back into the doorway butt naked with a smile on her face.

"Anything else?" she asked.

"Naw, that's it."

"Oh, I should probably grab this. This air feels cold out here after getting out of that hot water," she said, grabbing a towel off the hook and wrapping it around her waist, just above her butt. She went and got everything from downstairs. She was smiling as she took out the new bottle. She was so excited to have Steve there and not have to feel like they were rushed for any reason. She was enjoying every minute of this. Despite what he was going through, she was so happy to be able to be there for him and take care of him. She walked back up the stairs with the bottle in one hand and the plate in the other. She walked up to Steve, handed him the bottle, and set the plate of coke off to the side. When she removed her towel, Steve looked at her wet, sexy body. Her breasts were glistening with the water, and her pussy was perfectly shaven. She climbed in again, but this time in front of him, facing him.

He opened up the bottle and took a few drinks out of it, then set it down at the edge of the tub. After drying his hands with a towel, he rolled up a bill, and sniffed two lines off the plate. He pinched his nose and tilted his head back for a second before sniffing again.

Shila just stared at him. His body was so sexy to her, but she didn't want to come on too strong. She was going to let him lead the way even though her pussy had been wet, wanting him inside, ever since he had arrived earlier. Steve felt his heartrate increase, and a wave of energy came over him. The coke woke him right up, and even though it had been a terrible day, he was feeling good again. "Here. Drink some of this with me. Don't be a lame," he said to Shila while handing her the bottle.

"Boy . . . whatever," she said with a smile as she snatched the bottle out of his hands and took a drink. "This is so strong. I don't see how you're able to drink this straight. It burns my throat."

"Shake it off. You gone be alright," he replied, taking the bottle back from her and taking another drink.

"Give me your foot," she said, scooting to the side and getting ahold of his right foot. "I give a real good foot massage."

"You way too pretty to know how to give a good foot massage."

She took his foot in her hand and replied, "Pretty girls know how to give massages and cater to a man too. You'll see." She started to gently massage his feet and calves. Steve didn't know if it was the cocaine or the foot and leg massage that started to cause his dick to swell. He leaned his head back over the edge of the tub, and sunk lower into it, loving how it felt. Shila moved up to his thighs, and he jerked his leg a little when she got to his cut.

"Oops, sorry," she said, smiling. "I'll be careful around that spot." Her massaging his thighs and the feeling of her wet body on the inside of his legs had his dick rock hard. He laid there, accepting the massage gratefully. His whole body felt like it was melting, except for his dick, which he could feel pulsing with blood. He repositioned himself to move one of the powerful jacuzzi jets to a different spot on his lower back. Shila slid her hands up his thighs, and wrapped her hand gently around his rock hard dick then released it. "What do we have going on there?" she asked with a grin as she went back to massaging his feet. Part of Steve wanted to attack her, throw her on the floor, and fuck her mercilessly. Another part of him wanted her to just scoot up toward him, and sit on his dick and ride it until he came. His mind had transitioned from feelings of pain to thoughts of erotic pleasure. This bath, massage, and a couple lines were just what he needed to get him feeling right.

CHAPTER TWENTY-TWO

Shila got out of the jacuzzi and turned off the jets, causing the bathroom to get noticeably silent, then she helped Steve get to his feet. Once he was standing, he felt a little light headed, possibly from the hot water or from the drugs and liquor. Either way, he wasn't as steady on his feet as he thought he would be so she held him up while she dried him off and wrapped a towel around his waist. She followed him out of the bathroom into the bedroom where he collapsed on the middle of the bed. When he hit the bed, the towel came undone, revealing one of his butt cheeks. Shila had the bottle in her hand and looked down at him, then twisted the top off and took another drink. She made a face and shook her head. It was still too strong for her. She didn't know how Steve could take big drinks off the bottle like he did. "Turn over and scoot up a little. Lay on your back with your head on the pillows. I'm not done massaging your feet."

Steve did what he was told while Shila took another drink. "Let me put on a movie. What kind of movies do you like to watch?"

"It don't matter. I'll watch whatever. I'm chilling and I can barely see anyway," he said while laughing.

She laughed noticing him slurring his words again. She knew he was messed up. She put on a random movie while he did another line and took another drink. He was all smiles, which made her glad. Though she knew that this wasn't the best way to deal with problems, she knew that this wasn't how Steve normally was so she found him being all messed up funny. For now, she just wanted him to be happy and not worry about anything.

He was looking so sexy to her laying on her bed with his towel around his waist. He didn't even bother to try to retie the towel around his waist again, so it barely draped over his private area. He was so handsome to her. Her eyes looked at his abs, which were very visible. He was still in as good of shape as he was back in high school. Steve laid there feeling the liquor and the coke as the movie started to play. Shila dimmed the lights, and got down on the end of the bed. She started massaging his left foot, and Steve closed his eyes and drifted off.

"Let me know if it's too rough or too soft, okay?"

"That's perfect how you're doing it right now."

"Okay, good. Your feet are so soft. I'ma get some lotion." She got up and grabbed some good quality lotion that smelled like French vanilla. She squirted some on her hands and rubbed them together before going back to work on his feet. The liquor and coke had him buzzing. He was trying to stay up, but the massage felt so good he was almost falling asleep. She noticed him going in and out. When he would fade out and start breathing heavily, she would do something like move his leg or punch him gently in the foot to wake him back up. She didn't want him to fall asleep, at least not yet. She wanted to have sex with him or at least give him head. She kept going on his feet, and eventually he started snoring heavily. He had had a long day. She knew he was exhausted, but she was still going to make a move on him. She started rubbing his legs, making her way up to his private area. His dick started to rise slowly through the towel. She put her hand underneath the towel and rubbed it gently as she admired his face while he slept. His dick was soon fully erect. She moved the towel fully out of the way, revealing his manhood. She waited a few minutes to see if he would wake up, then she got down by his hips and wrapped her lips around his dick and begin licking it gently. She started moving up and down on his dick, sucking very slowly. All she wanted to do was make him feel good, and this was part of the presidential treatment package she felt he deserved after such a terrible day. She didn't remember his dick ever being this hard before. She kept going, and soon he woke up and his eyes grew wide as he saw what she was doing. He shook his head up and down, approving of what she was doing. That motivated her to try and fit his whole dick in her mouth. She tried to get it all in there gently, but wasn't successful.

"You can sit on it," he whispered in a sleepy voice. She was so happy to hear those words come out of his mouth. Her pussy was soaking wet. She climbed on top of him and slid his dick inside her and started riding him slowly. She had a rhythm going in her head that she rode him to and she made herself cum after only about three minutes.

She leaned forward and whispered in his ear, "This dick so hard and feel so good." She had his dick in the perfect spot for her, and she was able to orgasm repeatedly. Each time she came, Steve could feel her getting more and more wet. He was blown away by how little she was moving and still being able to make herself cum. He started to press his hips up into her with each move she made to see if she liked it.

"Ouu, baby. Yes, do that," she moaned, and after a few thrust of Steve's hips, she was cumming again. She twisted around on his dick and started bouncing her ass up and down. He watched his dick going in and out of her, and it turned him on. He could feel the pressure building inside himself.

"Oh, shit. I'm about to cum," he moaned as he thought about lifting her off of him to pull out. Shila didn't say anything and just started bouncing faster on him. "I'm about to cum in you," he warned her, but that's exactly what she wanted. She wasn't on birth control anymore and had started taking prenatal vitamins.

"Give me all of it, baby," she moaned as she kept increasing her speed, bouncing faster and faster. "Cum inside me."

"Oh, shit. Oh, shit. Yessss!" he moaned. "I'm cumming. Shit! Argggggggg!" he said, while his dick started exploding deep inside her. He had to grab her butt to slow her down. He pulled her hips down on him as his dick pumped out every last drop inside of her. Once he finished cumming, she looked back at him with a smile. "It's still hard. You want me to stay on?"

"Go ahead. Turn back around though, and move slow."

CHAPTER
TWENTY-THREE

The next morning, Steve woke up and looked at his phone. It was 8 a.m. and he had 77 missed calls. Angelia had been calling all night, and she was now calling once again. He shook his head, set his phone next to him, and laid back down. Shila was still asleep beside him butt naked. Her ass was facing him so he laid behind her wrapping his arms around her and resting his face in her sweet smelling hair. He cuddled her for a minute, then felt his dick start to rise. She pushed her butt back into him like she wanted it, so he slipped it inside her and started grinding up against her until he came. She laid there afterwards and he stood up.

"Where is the towels and stuff? I'm bout to take a shower."

"They are in the linen closet right next to the shower. Everything you need will be in there. There are toothbrushes, toothpaste, soap, shampoo, conditioner, and all that. Take whatever you need. If there is anything else you need for me to get you, just let me know."

"Okay. I'ma text you my size and shit so you can grab a few things for me today. I left everything in the house, and I'm not going back. Well, at least no time soon."

"Okay, I got you, boo," she said as she closed her eyes and went back to sleep.

Steve took a hot shower, which felt great. His neck was sore from the whiplash, and his whole back felt tight. He let the hot water run on his body and it felt much better afterwards. After the couple Tylenols he found in the medicine cabinet kicked in, he felt like a new man. He looked at Shila sleeping peacefully while he got dressed, then he went downstairs. It wasn't until he got to the kitchen when he realized that he didn't even have a car he could drive right now. He walked back upstairs and laid next to Shila. He gently woke her from her sleep.

"Damn, baby, I just realized I don't even have a car right now. Can you take me to grab a rental car real quick? I need you to put it in your name too since I don't have a credit or debit card."

"I can do that, but why don't you at least have a debit card?"

"I don't know. I just never took the time to open a bank account."

"Oh, naw. We about to go to the bank right now," she said, sitting up in bed. "It don't take that long to open up an account. You got some money you want to bring with you?"

"Yeah."

"Okay. Bring some with you, and we'll get you an account. You playing out here." She shook her head as she stood up. "You ain't even got a bank account? What are you doing? We gone get you together today. We can go to my bank and I'll get a $50 referral fee too." She walked her naked body to the bathroom, and Steve watched her ass jiggle as she brushed her teeth. Shila gave him a look. She knew what he was doing, and it made her laugh. She spit out her toothpaste and told Steve that she was jumping in the shower. She took a quick shower, and they were out the door in no time. Steve watched her as she drove to her bank. She really was beautiful, and she had it together. She had some black leggings on with a red shirt and a black hat straight to the front with a ponytail coming out the back. He didn't understand why he had wasted so much time with Angelia.

CHAPTER TWENTY-FOUR

When they got there, she went inside with him, and he opened up a checking and a savings account. He put $3,000 in checking and $4,500 in savings. The whole process was much easier than he thought it would be. The only thing he needed was an ID. They even issued him a debit card on the spot, and he was out the door on the way to the rental place.

"Damn, I shoulda been did that," he said, smiling and looking at the card with his name on it.

"I told you it was simple. I didn't bring you here because I was hesitant to put a rental in my name. I just wanted you to have a bank account. There is no reason for you not to have one."

"I know. I thought about it before, but never did it. You finally stopped me from procrastinating. That's cool. I like that. You get big points with me for that."

"Oh, really?" she said while she laughed.

"Yep. You looking good today with your lil' hat on. You got ready quick this morning too," he told her.

"Thanks, I try."

They pulled up to the rental place and parked. When he walked inside, Steve noticed a familiar face. "What up, my nigga?"

Chris smiled. "What's good? Long time no see. How you been?"

Chris and Steve were best friends back in the day when they were in middle school. They used to spend the night at each other's houses and play PlayStation all night long. They hadn't seen each other in a few years. "I been good. How about you?"

"I'm doing alright. Can't really complain."

"So this is where you're working? How's the family? I heard your ass got like 5 kids now."

Chris laughed. "Yeah, 5 with one on the way," he said as he shook his head.

"Damn, boy. You ain't playing out here."

"They got to eat too, man. It's hard out here. I just got this rental place under a franchise. It's been okay so far."

CHAPTER **TWENTY-FIVE**

"Oh, this your spot?"

"Yeah, they gave me 20 cars to start off with. I been doing it for about 6 months now. It's easy. I just come up here myself and I don't really do anything. I got a guy that cleans all the cars. I just basically be chilling, so I gotta get me a side hustle to keep me busy."

"Damn, that's dope. This is a nice setup too. What else you been into? You be fucking around in the streets?"

"Naw, not really. I been keeping a clean slate. I try to keep my ass out of trouble. I may fuck with some weed or something, but that's about it."

"Shit, we need to sit down and talk. I have an idea that may work out smooth for you where you don't need to do much at all. From what you saying, you pretty good at doing nothing," Steve said and they both laughed.

"Yeah, that would be sweet. We can sit down whenever you're free. You know I'm solid and gone keep shit tight for sure."

"Yeah, I know. I ran into your brother a couple months ago. He was telling me about you, saying you was doing good. He didn't mention this rental place though."

"Yeah, he was a little jealous of this move I made. You know he still in the streets and ain't got shit to show for it, so he kinda hating and shit."

"Tell that nigga to fuck with me. I can help him out. We can all get some money out here. I know you niggas solid. Set up a meeting, and we can figure something out."

Chris nodded and gave him a pound. "What you got going on anyway? You talking like you got a big bag or something."

"Shit, I do." Steve started laughing. "But hey, I need y'all just as much as I'm sure y'all need me."

"Shit, I can call him right now and see when he's free. We can set something up ASAP."

"Bet. I'm ready," Steve told him. "I need a whip though for about a week. What you got for me?"

"I got you. No worries. What you trying to jump in? Oh, you know I be building stash spots in cribs, cars, underground, or whatever too."

"Oh, yeah. We for sure gone get some money, trust me on that. Let me get something lowkey. I like that Chevy Traverse out there if that's available."

"Yeah, you can get that. I can give it to you for $225 a week."

"That's cool. Yeah, I'll take it."

"Wait until I tell Aubrey I finally seen my brother from another mother."

They exchanged numbers realizing they both still had each other's numbers from the last time they saw each other. Steve was just busy and had never called him. He actually remembered Chris calling him a few times, but he wasn't in a good place at the time.

"Tell Aubrey I said hello."

"I will. You know I live right here now," he said, pointing to the house right next door. "I literally work in my back yard."

"Damn, that's pretty cool, definitely a blessing." Chris handed Steve the keys and had him fill out the paperwork. After a few minutes, Steve was out the door. Steve planned to link up with him soon. He noticed that he had an opportunity with what Chris had going on. Chris had been trying to be cool with him forever, and now Steve was going to start dealing with him. He had never heard anyone speak a bad word on Chris ever. Everyone knew Chris was always pretty solid, and he always found a way to get money no matter what he did.

CHAPTER
TWENTY-SIX

Steve walked up to Shila and gave her a kiss on the lips. He thanked her for taking him to the rental place, and let her know that he ran into an old friend. He told her that he would be back to her place later. She could still see the hurt in his face. He was playing like everything was normal and trying to take care of his business, but she knew it would take some time.

"What you want to eat later? I can cook," she said as he was getting into the SUV.

He turned, looked at her, and pointed his finger at her. "You," he said, smiling and winking at her. She smiled and started blushing.

"No problem. If that's what you want to eat, I can set it on the table for you." She smiled again, got in her car, and drove off.

Steve left the rental place and headed over to Juice's house. When he got inside, Juice introduced him to the friend he had been knowing for years. His name was Cinco, and he had come all the way from New York to meet Steve. He moved a nice number of bricks every week. Juice plugged him in with Steve in return for Steve dropping his price $2,500 per brick. After a brief discussion, they all agreed to start doing business together. Cinco had brought enough money to pay for 50 kilos, but that made Steve nervous. After Cinco showed him the money, he asked to be excused, and walked outside with Juice.

"I appreciate what you doing for me and all, but you sure you know this nigga? He ain't the Feds or no shit, right?"

"Lil' bro, hell yeah I know this nigga. This nigga like my brother. He run some streets in New York, and I been knowing him for years. When I told him I had a plug for him and told him the price, he was interested. Since you my little bro, I'm like I might as well hook y'all up. Both of y'all solid. I couldn't make no money being in between y'all, so that was a no brainer for me. He respect me enough and ain't gone never do no messed up business with you. You have my respect too, so I know you ain't gone do no messed up business with him, so I think it can work. Dude ain't the Feds, bro. This nigga solid. He a cold killa and a money getta. He got a brother that you should meet too, but Cinco want to see how things go with you first. I gave him my word, and now I'm giving you my word. You ain't never got to worry about me or him crossing you, telling on you, none of that shit. We ain't the niggas that's telling, we the niggas that's killing. You know I ain't playing no games out here. This shit for real."

Steve looked at him then gave him a handshake and a hug. "Let's get this money," Steve said as he followed him back into the house. Steve sat down across the table from Cinco and they ironed out all the details. After everything was agreed upon, they locked things in. Both of them were ready to do business.

Steve left and drove back over to the rental place to talk to Chris. He knew he said he could build stash spots, but he wanted to check out how good he really was at it. Chris excitedly showed him two different cars he built stash spots in, but Steve wasn't impressed. He had seen way better ones. They were alright, but not good enough for what he was doing. Steve told him about the guy he knew who did stash spots, and asked him if he could do them on about 5 of Chris' cars. Chris agreed without hesitation, and then told Steve about the tunnel he had underground from the rental place to his house. He said that the last owner had it set up like that. Chris had purchased the house and the building from the owner as a package deal. Steve immediately tried to talk Chris into buying the house and building from him, but Chris didn't want to sell. He said he would be more than happy to work with him though and make some things happen. Chris wanted in on what Steve had going on.

CHAPTER **TWENTY-SEVEN**

Steve left the rental shop and drove the Traverse up to the shop in Detroit to have a stash spot put inside of it. It took him a while to get it done, but he waited, texting his mom, James, the twins, and a few others. Soon, a text was coming in from Shila.

Shila: I miss you already.

Steve: I'm coming back again. Just taking care of some business.

Shila: Yay! I can't wait. You smelled so good. What kind of cologne do you wear?

Steve: Lol I'm not telling you all that, sweetheart.

Shila: Whyyyyyyyyyy!

Steve: It's a special one. I don't want all your boyfriends wearing it.

Shila: You the only boyfriend I'm going to have.

Steve: Lol whatever.

Shila: I'm serious, Steve. Why you think I don't want to be with you?

Steve: I didn't say that.

Shila: Well, that's how you acting with me. You can open up with me. I'm not going to hurt you, I promise.

Steve: It ain't that. We good. I fucks with you for sure. I feel relieved to be away and spending time with you. You making this process easy for me and I appreciate that.

Shila: I know you need some time and I'm going to give you that, but you have to know that I'm trying to be yours for sure.

Steve: I'm not against that at all.

Shila: You have to stop nutting in me too. I'm not on birth control no more.

Steve: Fuck it. It is what it is. I ain't tripping.

Shila: So if I get pregnant, then what?

Steve: I'ma put yo' ass on child support.

Shila: LMAO I'm crying!

While Steve texted with Shila, Angelia was calling back to back. She had left him so many voicemails that his mailbox was full. She started sending him audio text messages, but he didn't care what she had to say, and he definitely didn't want to hear the sound of her voice. He planned to re-watch some of the videos of her to try and keep the same energy he had at the moment. He needed to reinforce the way he was feeling, and make sure he wouldn't do something dumb like take her back. He was still stressing and starting to feel like he didn't want to talk to anyone. Angelia started sending text messages again.

Angelia's texts:

-Wow! I can't believe you are doing me like this.

-I hope you don't think this is funny, avoiding me like this.

-When I start going crazy on your ass you're going to wish you answered and let me explain.

-Steve, please call me.

-Call me please.

-Just answer the phone. I need to talk to you for a few minutes.

-This is sickening how you can do this knowing I just told you I was pregnant.

-Answer the phone. It's important.

-So you don't want this baby?

-Call me.

-Where are you?

-I thought you loved me. This says a lot.

-Call me back.

CHAPTER
TWENTY-EIGHT

The next morning, Angelia rushed out of the house. She went up to Milan Federal Prison to talk to Steve's uncle. When Swift came out and saw her standing there, he was confused. He assumed it was Steve coming up to visit. "What's up?"

"Hi, I'm Angelia in case you don't remember me. I'm Steve's soon to be wife." She hugged him and they both sat down. He remembered her, but was really hoping she wasn't up there to tell him some bad news.

"Okay, you look lost, kinda nervous," she began. "I'm just here to talk to you because I'm in love with your nephew and I know you guys are really close. I figured you might be able to give me some advice or help me out."

He stared at her. He could tell she was nervous and that she had forced herself to come up there to talk to him. Although he had a lot of negative feelings about her based on what Steve had told him, he was going to at least listen to her and hear what she had to say. "How are you?" he asked. "I know who you are."

She smiled. "I'm doing good. I'm glad you remember me. So me and Steve been going through a lot and we really need some help."

He peered into her eyes, then leaned back in his chair and crossed his arms. "Well, from my understanding, you've been cheating on him. That got something to do with it?"

"Well . . . not really . . . I mean, okay, yeah, I cheated, but I apologized, and he forgave me for it. I cheated in the past and now it's like haunting me. He recently got ahold of some videos of me having sex with a guy, and now he's not talking to me. He's not answering the phone, returning messages, or nothing."

"Can you blame him?"

"Look, if you just going to take his side, I'm going to leave now and save my breath."

"Hold on. I'm not taking anyone's side. What's wrong is wrong. You haven't told me anything he did wrong yet. Being upset about seeing videos of his girl having sex with another man is understandable. You've only told me what you did wrong. What do you want me to say to what you've told me?"

"I'm pregnant with his baby. I don't feel like he should be doing this to me."

CHAPTER
TWENTY-NINE

He swallowed hard and took a deep breath. Pregnant is not what he wanted to hear. He knew Steve was going to end up getting her pregnant. It was only a matter of time. "So, he seen these videos of you and he's avoiding you now?"

"Yes! We have this big ass house. He didn't leave me any money to take care of any bills or nothing." She started to cry and her voice was cracking. "I know I messed up. I made some mistakes, but I swear I love and care for that man. We usually work things out, talk about them, and move on," she cried, and tears fell from her eyes.

"Well, that's part of the issue right there. You talk about it and move on. Are you guys actually fixing the issues or just burying them?"

"I thought it was fixed. I told him what I wanted. I told him the reason I was cheating. He changed a few things, and I'm okay with who he is. All these things keep coming up from my past though that he just can't seem to let go of."

"You said 'I' a few times. 'I told him, 'I' thought, 'I'm' okay . . . Did you listen to him or what he had to say?"

"Well, yeah, or at least I thought I did."

"How old are the videos? Are they from before you guys were together?"

"No, they were from while we were together."

"Plus you got caught having sex with a guy at the house?"

"He told you that?"

"Yep."

"Um, yes. I did."

"Let me ask you this. Does cheating twice, making a video, and getting caught red handed with a guy sound like a situation that would make it easy to forgive?" He asked her the question seriously, but calmly. He wasn't being smart with her. He was just trying to make her see it from another perspective.

Angelia sat there silently. She had been so focused on all the wrong things, and the gravity of what she had put him through was starting to hit her.

"If you caught him like that . . . with a girl in your house, and with a girl on video . . . wait, multiple videos while y'all was together . . . what would you do? Be honest."

"I would forgive him," she lied and continued crying.

"Well, if it was me, I wouldn't forgive you, but . . . I know that he definitely loves you. You seem like you love him too otherwise you wouldn't be up here. But you have to understand there is a lot of damage done and it will take some really hard work to get back in with him to where he actually trusts you again. There's no doubt in my head that you guys love each other. That's clear. But you guys need to learn how to treat each other. You don't do that kind of shit to someone you love and expect them to just take it."

"I know, but I didn't know what else to do. All Steve was doing was working all day every day. We was having sex like 6 times a month . . . maybe. He was going days without even touching me, so I thought he was cheating honestly."

"You didn't think to sit down and talk to him?"

CHAPTER **THIRTY**

"I tried, but he was always either falling asleep or saying how tired he was or how he didn't want to talk at the moment. I didn't want to leave him. I still don't want to be separated from him. I love him, but shit, I have needs. He is truly who I feel comfortable around. He is who I feel safe with. He spends a lot of time with me," she sniffed and wiped her eyes. "I mean . . . he's awesome. He really is. I'm so sorry for what I did. I just want him to forgive me so we can get married and have our kid and then make more babies." She smiled through her tears at the thought of having a family with Steve.

"I understand what you saying. I can hear the passion in your voice and see that you mean what you say. Look, my only advice is that when you know you want something, you gotta fight for it. Keep fighting for what you want. And I'm telling you this out of the goodness of my heart for y'all situation because I, personally, wouldn't dare take you back."

Her mouth dropped. "Dang, really?"

"Yeah, really." He sat there for a second before speaking so she knew he was dead serious. "I don't put up with no shit like that. At all."

"So you going to sit here and tell me you've never been cheated on by a woman?"

"Yeah, I have. I never said I didn't."

"Okay, and what happened?"

"I left her ass, plain and simple. I just told you I'm not dealing with any of that. You cheat once, you will do it again. That's how I feel, and all my years of living and experience as well as watching the people around me have proven that to be a fact."

"I disagree with that. I will never cheat on him again. And I can stand on that."

"I hear you, but that's going to be hard for certain individuals to believe. That's all I'm saying. Especially when it's already happened more than once."

"Sometimes people have to go through certain things to see and learn certain lessons. I know I have."

"I agree," he said as he pointed to himself. "Look at me. I'm in prison, so I understand trial and error. I understand making the wrong choices and learning from them. My nephew loves you a lot. Like I said, that much is clear. What I don't know is what decision he is going to make. I haven't heard from him, but I'm sure I'll be hearing from him soon."

"Can you please like call him when you get back there and tell him to meet with me so we can talk? Give me a chance to explain my side of the story face to face. We was just literally making love and now he won't respond to me. This is so crazy."

Swift didn't really know what else to say to her. He didn't think she was the one for Steve anyway, so he felt like he had done more than enough to help her out. He was fine if they didn't get back together. He could see that Angelia was a pretty girl with a nice body, but Steve was on a whole different level mentally, and he didn't sense that she was even close to wanting the same types of things out of life that he wanted.

"Just please can you talk to him for me? I mean, I don't want to waste your time with our problems. I know you have your own problems as well." She was so sad and didn't know what else to say or do. She could tell that Swift wasn't too much of a fan of hers, even though he had given her some advice. She could tell by how quiet he was being with her that he was only listening to her out of respect for Steve. "Thank you for listening. I'ma just go now. It was nice seeing you." She got up, still crying, and walked out of the visiting room. She was so irritated and embarrassed once she got in the car. Swift made her see some of her actions for what they truly were, disloyalty. She wished she hadn't even drove to Milan to visit him.

CHAPTER
THIRTY-ONE

Week Later

Shila and Steve were at a huge semi truck lot where they had brand new and used semi trucks for sale. They walked around looking at the new trucks, and Shila explained some of the different options that were important for Steve to know.

"So damn, all these new ones is $150,000-$200,000?"

"Yes, the brand new ones you'd want are right around there, plus tax of course," Shila replied.

"Damn, that's not even including the tax? Shit." Steve walked around a red truck that had caught his attention. When they checked out the inside, they saw that it had a double bunk, refrigerator, and all kinds of other cool features. Shila told Steve that she would buy the truck for him if he wanted it, and he could give her the dirty money to pay for it. Steve told her that he appreciated the offer, but he wasn't ready just yet. He wanted to do some more homework, and look into potential drivers first.

They walked and looked at some of the used trucks as well. There were some pretty nice used trucks that were in great condition that could save him some up front money. The whole time they looked around, Angelia called him and texted him nonstop. He shook his head as he felt his phone vibrate endlessly. When they finished looking at trucks, he pulled out the phone to see what type of crazy stuff Angelia was on today. After continuous pleas to have him call her, she had started to threaten him. Then she started to say that she was going to beat up Shila when she saw her whether he was with her or not. He scrolled through the messages, glad that he didn't have to be around her at the moment.

Before he put his phone away, one more text came through saying that if he didn't respond, she was going to surprise him. He still didn't respond. He had nothing to say to her right now. He was trying to just move forward with his life. Steve was setting up new things to make the kind of future he wanted.

Steve and Shila had been doing great. They were having sex like crazy. Three to four times a day was the normal for them. They couldn't be left anywhere alone without them being all over each other. Shila was making her best effort to keep Steve's mind off of Angelia, and she was doing a good job. Steve was staying busy and feeling pretty good. Steve's uncle had texted him about what happened with Angelia showing up, and told him a little about the conversation they had. Steve promised his uncle that he would come up there to visit him soon. For now, he was taking care of business. He had the whole rental operation set up with Chris. They had five different vehicles with stash spots built into them. Each car could hold large volumes of product. Steve had brought everything to Chris' house, which nobody knew about, and it was working out very well.

Cinco was getting 50 kilos at a time, and loving the service he was getting. He didn't even have to pay up front anymore. He would pay Steve whenever he would bring the car back. This service was only for his top five people that were moving product for him. These were the people that he knew well, including their families. Everybody was exceeding Steve's expectations, and the business grew quickly. The money was coming in fast.

CHAPTER THIRTY-TWO

It had been about a week and a half since Steve had spoken to Angelia. Esha and Candy had both called him. He actually answered their calls and took the time to speak to each of them individually. He spoke to them about how he felt. He vented to them and even cried over the phone to both of them about what had happened and how bad he was hurt. They listened to him, but they had a single-minded mission of getting him and Angelia back together no matter what, so they weren't really trying to be sympathetic to what he was saying. They didn't care whether Angelia was wrong or right, they just wanted them back together. Steve just told them that he needed some time to think and get things back in order because he had been slacking on important things.

About 7 o'clock in the morning, Steve woke up to his phone vibrating. Angelia's messages had slowed down, so he was actually checking his phone regularly again. He looked at the message. It was from Angelia. He almost just closed it, but he saw it was a video. When he clicked on it, it was a video of his house on fire. The boat that he had just bought was on fire too. "What the fuck!" he yelled as he jumped up, scaring Shila awake.

"What happened?" she asked, still half asleep. "You okay?"

Steve didn't say anything. He just ran out of the room in his boxers and called Angelia. His heart was beating fast. The phone just rang and rang. After trying to call her twice, he sent her a text.

Steve: What the fuck happened?

Angelia: I don't know. The house caught on fire.

Steve: Why are you not answering the phone?

Angelia: I'm talking to the police.

Steve: How did the house catch on fire? Then the boat is on fire too! How the fuck did that happen? I don't even have insurance on that boat yet.

Angelia: All you care about is money. You not going to ask me if I got out safe or not? You talking about this stupid ass boat.

Steve: Stupid ass boat? You the one that wanted the damn boat. You are clearly okay. You're not in there.

Angelia: Whatever. So this is the only way to get a response from you, huh?

Steve: How?

Angelia: Something bad happening. I heard you been dealing with Shila too. It's going to be a war when I see her.

Steve: Call me when you can talk on the phone.

Angelia: Oh now you want to talk?

Steve: I'm trying to see about your well being. And where you going to go since this house den burned down?

Angelia: You don't care about my well being, Steve. I don't even think you care about me. It's been weeks since you have talked to me at all. I thought different about this relationship, but now I see where I stand. You left me for dead, knowing I don't have money, knowing I can't afford to pay the bills at this house, knowing that I'm pregnant with your baby and all. You're going to regret that you ever did me like this, nigga.

Steve: What about what you did to me?

Angelia: We both did shit.

Steve: You did way more though. Way more. And I only did shit after you did.

Angelia: I been trying to talk to you all week about this shit but you been ignoring me, so fuck you and your slut ass bitch.

Steve: Oh, now it's fuck me? All you do is try to manipulate and reverse shit. I caught onto your games now since I had a chance to think.

Angelia: Where you been, Steve? Why can't we meet up?

Steve: Because every single time I'm around you, you talk me into forgiving you after you did some fucked up shit. It's always the same shit with you.

Angelia: It's called LOVE. We love each other and that's why we forgive each other. You bet not be with her. Are y'all together, Steve?

Steve: Naw. Would it even matter if we was?

Angelia: If the bitch was dead, would it matter?

Steve: Why you talking crazy?

Angelia: You haven't seen crazy.

Steve: Wow.

Angelia: Can we meet today please? I need to see you and talk to you in person.

Steve: What time? And where?

Angelia: I'll let you know what hotel I'm going to be at later. The renter's insurance is covering me for a little while, but I'm supposed to do a video to make some money. I can't believe you left me this fucked up, Steve. This is so fucked up.

Steve: Just let me know where you gone be when you figure it out.

Angelia: Okay.

CHAPTER THIRTY-THREE

Steve came back upstairs and sat on the edge of the bed. He stared at the wall, and didn't know what to do next. He was pissed off about the house, and especially the boat since he didn't have insurance on it yet. He thought that Angelia started the fire, but he didn't know for sure. Shila woke up and saw him staring off into space. "Is everything okay?"

"Yeah, everything is cool. I guess Angelia burned the house down that we was living in," he said, still staring off at nothing.

"What? On purpose or was it an accident?"

"I don't know. I was texting her. I can't tell. I'm not exactly sure what the fuck happened, but she needs money."

"And?"

"I was gonna maybe take her some money."

"For what? Fuck that broke ass bitch!" Shila said as she stood up and faced Steve. He looked up at her. "She messed up and cheated on you. You don't owe her shit!"

"She's pregnant with my baby. I ain't about to just leave her out in the cold," he said, holding his arms out like he didn't have a choice in the matter.

Shila shook her head. She had a lot on her mind that she wanted to say. She caught herself though and held her tongue since it was still early with her and Steve. She didn't want Steve to get mad at her and leave over her saying something crazy.

"Why can't you have your mom give it to her, or your friend James? He would do that for you."

"What's wrong with me giving it to her?"

"You bet not have sex with her, Steve," she said, bending over to look him in the eyes.

"What the fuck?" Steve said, standing up and putting his hands around Shila's waist. "Why would I have sex with her? That's not even on my mind. Stop overthinking shit."

Shila wrapped her arms around him and looked up at him. "You promise?"

"Promise? Are you serious?"

Shila took a step back from him. "Yeah, I'm serious, Steve. That bitch is something else. There is no way I will ever trust her."

"Just relax, please. Let me take care of what I need to take care of," he said, leaning in and giving her a kiss on the lips before walking into the bathroom. Shila laid down on the bed and watched him get ready.

As soon as he left Shila's place in his Ram truck, Chris called him to let him know that three cars had just been returned. For Steve, that meant it was time to go pick up some money. He had about 75 kilos left, and he knew he had to go see his uncle so he could let him know that he wasn't with Angelia. Hopefully he'd let him work with Karo again. He planned to pay Karo this week for the last shipment he got.

CHAPTER **THIRTY-FOUR**

Steve wasn't looking forward to meeting up with Angelia, because he already knew she'd be on some type of nonsense. He pulled up at the rental place, stepped out, met with Chris, and picked up a few duffle bags of money. He made sure he took out Chris' share of the cash to pay him. Steve had a lot to take care of, so he didn't hang around and chill. Within 5 minutes, he was out the door and back in his truck. While he was waiting to turn out of the parking lot, he saw a white Ram dually truck with a logo that read 'Amilli Trucking' on it. He instantly thought about the author, A. Roy Milligan, and he wanted to honk his horn. He wanted to get his attention, but didn't want to come across like a maniac. He pulled out behind him since he was going to be heading in the same direction anyway, and he followed him, hoping he would come to a stop somewhere public. Within a mile, the white Ram pulled into a do-it-yourself car wash. Steve pulled in behind him, and parked next to him. Steve saw him get out of his truck, and he walked toward him to introduce himself.

"Hey, what's up? You the one that wrote the Car Hauling book?"

"Yeah, that's me. You checked it out?"

They shook hands and greeted each other. "Yeah, I read it. It was helpful as hell. I'm thinking about getting some trucks myself. I was just looking at some and wondering what I should get. You have any recommendations?"

"Well, are you going to be driving it or getting a driver to work for you?"

"Getting a driver."

"Are you going to be doing long distance runs out of state or will you be staying local?"

"Which ones pay the most?"

"Well, probably the state to state."

"Okay, then I'm doing state to state."

"So you will definitely want to get a truck with a sleeper on it for sure. If you had a nice local contract that paid decent you could get a day cab instead. That's what I have right now, since my drivers are local."

"The day cab is still a semi, right? It just don't have a sleeper on it and it's the one where the driver look like he sitting straight up?"

Roy laughed. "Yep, that's the one."

"Are those cheaper than a sleeper?"

"They are."

"Okay, so how many trucks you recommend me to start off with?"

"Shit, how many drivers you have that's ready to roll?"

"None right now, but I was actually heading over to my cousin's house to see if he wants to get his license and drive for me."

"Oh, okay. That's cool. Understand this too . . . when you are a new driver, the insurance will start off higher than usual, but after you've had your license for a while, it will go down."

"Oh, so like if I get an experienced driver the rate will be different?"

"Yeah, way different, especially if they have a good driving record with no tickets or anything like that. But, like I said in the book 'From Prison to the Car Hauling Game', Michigan is one of the states, maybe like one of the top 3, with the highest insurance rates in the United States. To get around that, you may want to switch your company address to a state with better rates. That can cut your rate in half, if not more than that."

"Yeah, I read that in your book. That's weird how each state has their own rates."

"I know, right? I switched everything over. I bought a crib in Ohio and that's my new residence. It don't make sense to pay them high ass prices when you don't have to. If you Google 'states with low insurance rates' it will tell you which states have the best rates and you can decide what you want to do from there. That shit really matters. Your insurance rate can go from $25,000 a year to $11,000 just by switching states."

"I feel you. So that's why you have Ohio plates?"

"Yup. Everything I own does. That's where I live now. It's only a couple hours away from here. I can always come here if I need to, but I ain't about to give them all my money to live here. Fuck that."

"Damn, I feel that. That's pretty cool. You got me thinking about how I should do my shit when I get set up. I heard refrigerated pays good. You know anything about that?"

"Yep, that pays real good. I got a guy I can hook you up with if you trying to do that. He go from Houston, Texas to New Jersey, dedicated route. He makes $12,000 a week."

"Damn, yeah, that sounds cool. What do I need to do?"

"Well, if you hook up with him, he has extra trailers and he'll probably let you run under his authority, so all you will have to do is get your own truck and driver. You can buy your own trailer too if you want. But if not, he will rent one to you that he owns."

"I'll buy a truck and then call him up for sure." Roy gave Steve the guy's number and told him to give him a call. Roy also exchanged numbers with Steve and told him to give him a call if he had any questions about anything. They both washed their trucks, and Steve left the car wash. When he pulled out onto the road, he called the number Roy gave him right away.

"Hello."

"Hey, this is Steve. I'm looking for Greg."

"Speaking. What's up, Steve? You the guy Roy just texted me about? He said you'd be calling."

"Yeah, that's me. How you doing?"

"I'm doing well. How are you?"

"I'm good. I was just thinking about getting into the trucking industry. He said you was doing refrigerated stuff so I just wanted to know if I could get a truck and somehow run under your authority?"

"Yeah, that can work. I charge 20 percent. The route I have runs from Houston, Texas to New Jersey every week. You will get about $12,000 a week, and I will take 20 percent of that. That will cover insurance, the electronic log fees, your IFTA and all that stuff. You have an email address? I'll send over a contract. The contract will lay out the specifics of everything that is covered in my 20 percent and if you're interested, you can let me know. I'm ready when you're ready. What kind of truck do you have?"

"Well, I'm going to buy one. Which one do you recommend?"

"Get one with a lot of horsepower. I drive Peterbuilts myself. 575 horsepower."

"Okay, I'm going to get a Peterbuilt then." Greg also told him what kind of trailer he recommended for him. Steve was really impressed with everything Greg was telling him. Steve told him that he would review the contract, and let him know when he is ready. When Steve hung up the phone, he received a text message from Angelia telling him what hotel she was staying at along with her room number. She told him to stop by whenever.

CHAPTER
THIRTY-FIVE

Steve decided to go ahead and meet up with Angelia now rather than put it off until later. He drove to the hotel in silence while his mind raced with all the things he wanted to say to her. He walked quickly across the parking lot straight inside and up to her room. He knocked, and she opened the door and stepped to the side without even speaking.

"Damn, what's wrong with you?" Steve asked.

"You really going to ask me that?"

"Yeah, why you got an attitude already?"

"You just disappeared on me like you don't care nothing about me. You ever think that maybe that's why I got an attitude?"

"Stop it. You know I care about you."

"The way you left, I can't tell at all," she replied, walking to the far side of the hotel room and staring out the window.

Steve walked about halfway across the room and explained, "I didn't know what else to do. I mean, what you want me to do? That shit hurt me."

"That's old, Steve. We already was moving forward."

"But it's new to me. Like, how many niggas have you slept with since we been together?"

"Just them two, and I regret it. I'm sorry, Steve, but let's fix this. I have your baby in my stomach," she said, turning to face him and putting her hands on her belly.

Steve was silent. He just looked at her.

Angelia continued, "How can we fix this? I'm going crazy. I'm missing you and wondering who you with, what you doing, who you laying with, and who you giving your attention to. Are you over me that fast? You haven't even tried to talk to me."

"I'm not doing any of the stuff you just mentioned. I love you, but you constantly keep showing me that I can't trust you. I'm out here putting my life and freedom on the line for you. I've been trying to make this work."

"I didn't tell you to start selling drugs, Steve."

"It's clear that you like a certain type of nigga. Niggas that's in the streets, getting money. That's what you like."

"How could you say that and I been with you when you didn't have shit?"

"But you was cheating on me with street niggas with money when I didn't have shit. It's street niggas with money. Don't tell me that ain't what you want."

"It's not about the money, trust me."

Steve just shook his head, then sat down in the chair at the desk, and turned to face her. "Then what is it about? Why would you make a video with a nigga? You know how stupid that made me look?"

"I'm sorry. I didn't look at it like that. I was hurt at the time when I did all that shit."

"Why didn't you come to me and talk to me about it?"

"I felt like you was just working and not going to be interested in nothing I had to say. You wasn't even touching me. It was like you was disgusted by me or something. I didn't know what to do, but I know that I wanted to feel wanted. So . . . I did stupid shit. I regret it so much now," she said, then broke down in tears. "I swear, Steve. It's nothing else to come after those videos," she sobbed. She sat down on the bed and bent over with her head in her hands, crying uncontrollably.

Steve looked at her for a minute, then got up and sat next to her and put his arm around her. He didn't really know what else to say or do. He felt hurt over the whole thing, but a part of him felt sad for her as well.

"Your uncle hates me," she told him.

"You talked to my uncle?" he asked as if he didn't already know.

"Yes, but he just stared at me the whole time like I was full of shit. I went up there to see him and talk to him and ask for his advice." She tried pulling herself together and fighting back the tears so she could have a conversation. "I know I messed up bad. I know I did, but I don't know what to do now. I'm so sorry, Steve. I swear, I'm so sorry for hurting you."

CHAPTER
THIRTY-SIX

Steve started to feel worse, and his eyes watered a little. He was having flashbacks to scenes in the videos while he looked at her. He tried to fight back the tears, but wasn't successful and a few of them fell. Angelia got up and went to the bathroom to get tissue to blow her nose and dry her eyes. Steve watched her as she walked back toward him, trying to hold it together. He could tell she was hurt, and if he was honest with himself, he had missed her this whole time even though Shila had been keeping him distracted.

Angelia was attractive to him. There was just something about her that always made him weak. She came and sat down on the bed next to him. Steve looked over at her as she looked back at him. It was in that very moment that Steve realized the only way he could possibly ever get over her was to stay away from her. She had some kind of raw, seductive power that would suck him in whenever he was around her.

"What happened with the house? How did it catch on fire? And the boat too?"

"I needed money, so I did a renter's insurance job. And I lit that boat on fire because I was pissed, okay?"

"Why didn't you just tell me you needed money?"

"I tried to, but you didn't answer."

Steve looked at the floor and thought for a minute. He didn't believe her and he was feeling the irreversible loss of trust in her once again. "I don't know if I can forgive you for all this shit to be honest with you."

Angelia's eyes filled with tears again and she put her head down. "What am I supposed to do? I need you, Steve. You all I have," she cried, getting on her knees on the floor in front of him. "Please, Steve. Just give me one last chance. On my dead grandma, I'll never hurt you again. I promise!" she sobbed, grabbing his leg. "I love you. I'm in love with you! You can't leave me like this. Look at me." Tears ran down her face as she looked up at him.

Steve got off the bed, and held her as she sat back against the wall. He didn't know what to do. He felt like shit for not answering any of her calls and just cutting her off the way he did.

"Baby, get up off this floor," he said, standing up and taking her by the hands to help her up.

Angelia wiped the tears off her face with her other forearm as he pulled her to her feet. They stood there just staring at each other, not saying a word for several minutes. Steve took off his shoes and laid back on the bed. Angelia just stood there staring at him. Steve laid there looking up at the ceiling, not knowing what he wanted to do. He could tell that she was sorry, and he felt bad for her. Another part of him felt like they had already been through this before.

Angelia walked around to the other side of the bed and just stood there looking at Steve while tears fell slowly down her face.

"What?" Steve asked. "Why you looking at me like that?"

"Can I at least lay down next to you, Papi?" she asked, standing there.

"Whatever, yeah, come on."

Angelia slid onto the bed and laid down next to him. She put her head on his shoulder, and they just laid there saying nothing for about fifteen minutes. He ran his fingers through her hair, and she kept her arm across his chest. Eventually, she started running her finger on his chest, followed by his stomach. Steve glanced down at her, but he couldn't see her face. Her head was still resting on his shoulder. Her finger ran just below his waistline, and back up again. He knew what she was trying to do, but he didn't do anything to stop it. Before he knew it, she had his dick out and she was sucking it. That led to an hour of hot, steamy make up sex. They attacked each other like starving hyenas eating a carcass. It was clear that they both had missed each other terribly.

After they were finished, Steve gave her $10,000 to find a place to stay. In addition to the money he gave her, she had a decent check coming from the renter's insurance.

"What are you about to do?" she asked him.

"All I know is I'm taking a shower. After that, I'm not sure." Steve went into the bathroom and locked the door behind him. He took a long, hot shower, crying through most of it. He didn't know what he should do now. He knew that he couldn't be around Angelia without that happening, but he didn't make any effort to stop it either. His mind thought about Shila, who had been treating him so well and giving him all the time he needed to recover from the heartbreak. He got out of the shower and dried off, throwing on the same clothes. He let Angelia know that he had some other business he needed to take care of. He could tell she wanted to say something, or ask questions about where he was going, but she kept quiet and just gave him a kiss goodbye.

CHAPTER THIRTY-SEVEN

When Steve left the hotel, he drove over to his cousin's house. When he pulled up in front of the house, his cousin Randy came out and jumped in the truck. "What's up with you?" Randy asked.

"Shit, what's going on with you? What you got going on out here?"

"Looking for a job, but ain't nobody hiring. My mom was saying you had something for me possibly?"

Steve nodded his head and said, "Yeah, possibly. Truck driving. What do you think about that? You ever thought about driving big trucks?"

Randy thought to himself for a second. Truck driving wasn't something that had ever crossed his mind. "Naw, not really. I never thought about it."

"I think it would be good for you. You ain't doing nothing else. You got kids yet?"

"Nope."

"Well, that's even better. I can buy a truck and you can drive it. We can get this money together. I'll pay you good."

Randy was only 18 years old, and had just graduated from high school. "Don't I have to go to school and get some kind of special license or something like that?"

"Yeah, I'm going to pay for all that. All you got to do is show up and do the work."

"Them trucks big as hell, man!"

Steve laughed. "That's a good thing. That means you gone be safe and secure while driving it. Everybody get scared when they driving on the side of a huge truck. I know I be getting the fuck out the way," he said.

They were both laughing when they noticed Randy's sister, Tory, walk outside and start coming towards them. "Why you be acting funny, Steve?" she said, rolling her eyes and sticking her head through the passenger window. She was standing on the foot rail and holding onto the door.

"Ain't nobody acting funny with you."

"Why you ain't come in and speak to me then?" Tory said, tilting her head and giving him a look.

"I ain't know you was in there. Dang, calm down."

"Naw, because you be acting funny. You never be reaching out to me or nothing."

"I be working all the time. I'm not acting funny."

"Hm, hm, what y'all talking about?"

"Get your nosey ass out of here," Randy said, pushing her off the side of the truck. She opened up the back door and jumped in.

Steve laughed as he turned around to the back seat to look at her. "We talking about truck driving. I'm trying to get Randy to drive a truck for my company."

"Ouu, I want to drive trucks!"

Randy and Steve laughed.

"What's so funny? I'm being serious. I really want to. I've seen girls drive trucks and my friend's mama and her daddy got their own truck. They are always on the road. They got that money too!"

"So, if I pay for you to go to driving school, you are ready to go?"

"Yes! Right now, I'm ready. I swear fo' God I'm ready."

"Hold on, hold on. He asked me to drive for him first," Randy interrupted.

"Y'all both can. I'll get two trucks," Steve assured them. "So, Randy, you want to drive for sure?"

"Yeah, I'm in."

"Okay, I'll get y'all both in class tomorrow. Y'all both got regular licenses right?"

"Yep," they both said in unison.

"Okay, so here's what's going to happen. Later, I'm going to send you the address to a trucking school in Detroit. When you get there, it'll already be paid for. You gotta take the class. Once you pass, call me, and we gone work."

"How long is the class and how much it cost?"

"About 3 weeks and about $2,500."

"Okay, bet," Randy said, nodding his head. He thought that it would've been much longer.

Steve laughed. "Tory, I swear this nigga ain't want to drive trucks until you came out here saying you wanted to drive them."

They all started laughing together.

"He lying. I was just thinking about it for a second."

"He always copying what I do," Tory said, laughing and pushing her brother. Randy and Tory were only one year apart. Tory was 19, and she was a lot more driven and motivated than her brother. She always did well in school and stayed busy with sports. Randy was a good guy, he just needed a little more external motivation. Steve sat and talked with them both for about 15 minutes. When he left, he called up the trucking school and paid for his cousin's classes, then was on his way to a restaurant in West Bloomfield to meet up with Shila.

CHAPTER
THIRTY-EIGHT

He made it to the restaurant before Shila did, and just sat in his truck listening to music and checking his phone. There were a handful of other cars sitting in the parking lot. He glanced up from his phone to see Shila pulling into a parking spot a few away from him. To his surprise, he saw Angelia in her car coming to a stop right behind Shila. Angelia got out of the car with a crowbar in her hand, and walked up to the driver's side window of Shila's car.

Steve's eyes got wide, and he jumped out of the truck and started running toward Angelia. By the time he got there, Angelia had smashed the crowbar through Shila's window, and Shila was out of the car swinging. "What the fuck are you doing?" he yelled, trying to pull Angelia away from Shila, but she had ahold of Shila's hair.

"Bitch, I'ma kill you!" she screamed, swinging and scratching at Shila.

"Let my hair go, hoe!" Shila shouted back, connecting a punch on Angelia's cheek that knocked her to the ground. By this time, there were three or four people standing around recording the action with their phones.

"World Stars!!!" a girl shouted, holding her phone up.

Steve was now in between them and had them separated, but Angelia still wanted a piece of her. "Chill out! What the fuck is wrong with you?" Steve shouted.

"Why you fucking with this bitch!" Angelia yelled, slapping Steve. "This where the fuck you been?"

"Bitch, don't worry about us!" Shila yelled back.

"I just got done fucking him, bitch! And I'm having his baby, bitch!"

"Bitch, I'm having his baby too, hoe!" Shila shouted.

Steve was pulling Angelia away from Shila, trying to get in her car so she could leave before someone called the police. Luckily the few people that were recording the incident seemed to be much more interested in the excitement than calling the police. Steve opened Angelia's car door and pushed her in there. She closed the door and drove out of there, holding her middle finger out the window.

Shila looked at her window. "I'm not getting in there with all that glass all over my seat. That bitch busted out my window."

"Well, either way we leaving, so you can ride with me," Steve said.

"Let me grab my stuff." Shila fixed her hair and straightened her bra. She got her purse and her phone out of her car and got in Steve's truck. "Crazy ass bitch. I'ma fuck her up when I see her!"

Steve didn't respond. He just started the car and backed out of his parking spot. As he was about to turn out of the restaurant parking lot, he saw Angelia's car driving directly at them. She crashed into the passenger side of his truck right where Shila was sitting, causing the airbag to deploy.

"This bitch crazy!" Shila yelled as she pulled her gun out of her purse. She shot two times through Angelia's windshield.

"What the fuck are you doing?" Steve shouted, reaching his hand out to try and stop Shila. Soon, five or six shots came back at them, and Shila caught three of them, one in the neck, one in the stomach, and one in the shoulder. Steve looked at Shila in horror as she grabbed at her neck while blood ran out between her fingers. Angelia threw her car in reverse and sped off in her wrecked car.

CHAPTER
THIRTY-NINE

5 Days Later

Steve was once again overwhelmed by his life, and the only thing he could think to do was go see Swift. He needed some guidance and advice on what he should do. It was a smooth, traffic-free drive out to the prison. When he got inside the visiting room, it was fairly empty. He sat there waiting for a few minutes before he saw his uncle come walking toward him with a big smile. He gave Steve a hug then sat down across from him.

"Talk to me, nephew," Swift said. He could see the pain and heartache all in Steve's face. Steve looked like he hadn't slept in days.

"Shit, I don't know where to start," Steve said, shaking his head.

"Well, let me start off for you. Are you alive and well? You above ground and breathing?"

"Yes."

"Good," he said with a nod. "And your mom? How is she?"

"She's good."

"How is your girlfriend? She came up to see me, last week I think it was."

"How did that go?"

"It went good. I just let her talk really. She had a lot to say, but I don't like her still. I think she's a liar so I didn't want to waste my breath on her. I do think she loves you and I think she was making some bad decisions for sure though."

"So remember the girl I was telling you about that had her shit together and had the dump trucks and all that?"

"Yeah, that's the one I liked for you. I remember you telling me about her."

"Well . . . I started dealing with her pretty tough after me and Angelia had broke up this time. Her name is Shila. The two of them got into a fight at a restaurant I was meeting Shila at. Well, let me slow down. Okay, so I went to go talk to Angelia after avoiding her because she sent a video of the house we was living in on fire. The boat I had bought was on fire too in the video."

"She den burned the house down?"

"Yes. She told me she did that because I left her with no money and I didn't talk to her for almost two weeks. She did it for some kind of job on the renter's insurance. She lit the boat on fire too because she was mad, but I didn't have insurance yet on that. I don't even know what she told the police. It looked like someone did it on purpose, so I don't know."

Swift shook his head. "That girl is nuts."

"I'm not even done yet. So, I went to go meet her to give her some money to hold her over. She has my baby and shit. So we had sex, I couldn't resist her of course. I took a shower, and while I was in the shower, I heard a door close like she left out or someone came in. I didn't really think much of it at the time. Later on, I was meeting up with Shila, the chick you like. We was meeting up at a restaurant. I showed up there first, and I swear I thought I saw Angelia's car at one point, but I ignored it. Once Shila pulled up, she was on her ass."

"How did she know you was gone be there?"

"That's what I'm saying, I don't know. I'm thinking she put a tracker on my whip when I was in the shower at the hotel room."

Swift laughed. "I can definitely see her doing that for sure. I'm telling you what I know. That girl is nuts!"

"I know. I see that now. Hold on a minute and let me finish telling you this shit. She goes up to Shila's truck. She has a brand new Benz SUV. She blocks her in and walked up to her window with a crowbar and smashes her window then starts whooping her ass. I had to run over there and stop the shit. They pulling each other's hair out and cursing each other out, talking about both of them pregnant and all."

"Damn, you got both of them pregnant?"

"Angelia I know for sure, yes. But Shila is late, almost two weeks late, for her period too. I found a prenatal vitamin bottle in the drawer so I think she was trying to get pregnant. This shit crazy man."

Swift was laughing hysterically and shaking his head.

"Anyway, I break them up and carry Angelia to her car and made her pull off. I go back to get Shila together. She has a couple scratches on her and her hair was all over the place, but nothing serious. Since her window is busted out, we go to my whip and get ready to leave . . . Man! Angelia came crashing into the side of my truck with her car like she really trying to kill this girl. She hit us hard too. Like the airbags deployed and everything."

"What the fuck?"

"Shila instantly got out her gun and shot into the car. They both have a license to carry. Shila's shots went through her windshield. Angelia shot back five or six times and hit Shila three times, one in the neck, one in the stomach, and one in the shoulder."

"Wow! Are you serious?"

"Yes."

"Is she alive? Is she okay?"

Steve shook his head. "She's in critical condition. She's not dead, but they saying she's going to be paralyzed from the shot in her neck. It hit her spine and did damage to the spinal cord, I guess, and they don't think she gone ever walk again."

"What happened to Angelia?"

"She sped off trying to get away and they caught her. She in jail on attempted murder charges and some other shit too."

"Wow, that's some crazy ass shit. What's wrong with that girl? She do drugs or something?"

"I don't know. I don't think so."

Swift shook his head. "So have you seen Shila since all this happened?"

"Yeah, I've been up at the hospital over the last three or four days with her whenever her kids and mom ain't there. I been up there just sitting and reading books and shit. I did get Angelia a lawyer. I've been talking to the lawyer and he said he could get her out on bond with a tether for $50,000 more. I already gave him $50,000 though. Her bond will be at least 250K, but I can go through the bail bondsman and get her out for $25,000."

CHAPTER **FORTY**

Swift nodded his head, but didn't say anything.

"What you think I should do? I mean you sitting there looking at me like I'm doing something wrong. She has my baby. I don't want her to just stay in there."

"I didn't even say anything about what you was doing."

"Why you looking at me like that then?"

"I was just thinking about something," Swift said, then paused for a minute. "You know that because Angelia shot back, she actually could have hit you too. I don't think she cared at that moment who she hit. You never fire rounds in the direction of someone you love. So I'm just glad that you wasn't hit. Both of you guys could have been dead. She shot 5 or 6 times at you and her. It only take two bullets to kill both of you, so it's a blessing that you are okay."

Steve nodded his head. "Yeah, that shit was unreal. It happened so fast too. I'm like what the fuck. Even when I seen Shila grab the gun, I reached out like I wanted to stop her, but it happened so fast I couldn't do shit."

"Damn."

"Yeah."

"So you got these girls out there going crazy trying to kill yo' ass, I see."

Steve shook his head. "Angelia called a few times crying and shit. She's not eating in there and wants to come home."

"She not eating yet? Don't worry, she'll be eating soon when she knows she has to eat."

"Yeah, I guess you right about that."

"So, what's going on with Karo? You paid her for the last load yet?"

"About that . . . I have the money together, but I need that plug back, Unk. I got these guys that's buying some heavy shit from me. Plus, I got a rental spot where I do the transactions and shit at. I just bought a motel too."

"You bought a motel? What kind of motel?"

"It looks like it was maybe a Motel 6 back in the day. It has 30 rooms, It's nice, just needs some work. James and a couple of his buddies are over there right now, building me some secret spots in it so I can stash my shit in there."

Swift started to grin and shook his head up and down while folding his arms and sliding back in his seat. "So you den took shit to a new level I see. No wonder Karo was asking if I was sure I wanted to cut you off. You been doing a good job for her obviously."

"For you, Unk . . . I have a half of a million stacked up. I was gonna drop that off soon for you."

Swift was shocked. "Damn."

"I been putting this shit together, and I still look normal out there. I ain't been flashy or nothing. I don't care about all that stupid shit. Clothes, cars, chains, and shit."

"Yeah, I know you don't care about that type of shit. That's one of the reasons I didn't mind hooking you up with Karo. I knew you wouldn't make shit hot by being flashy and shit."

"Naw, I'm on some other shit. Buying clothes, jewelry, cars and shit . . . that's little nigga shit to me. I'm not even trying to sound arrogant, but I'm no little kid. I need real shit out here in these streets especially if I'm risking my freedom and my life for it. So, I don't be spending shit. Angelia was the one wanting all that flashy shit. She the one that be wanting people to know she got money."

CHAPTER FORTY-ONE

Swift shook his head. "Yeah, the stories you told me about her made me nervous. I didn't want her to have you in the middle of some bullshit."

"Yeah, I know. She gone be on house arrest now. So what you think about me getting back on with Karo? I've already shown her what I can do, and now the way I'm set up . . . everything is ready to go."

Swift could see the passion in his eyes. Steve didn't want to stop growing and diversifying his businesses. He loved coming to see uncle Swift and was still wearing the same pair of shoes he was wearing the very first time he visited him.

"Since she gone be on tether, we can keep it going. But keep her out of your business, and I mean that. I don't trust her at all. I know you love her, but I would feel very uncomfortable with you dealing with Karo with Angelia on the loose. Since she's on house arrest, she shouldn't be right up under you so it should be fine."

Steve could see that Swift was serious about what he was saying. He didn't want Angelia anywhere near his business. "Thanks, Unk. I appreciate that," he said, giving him a hug.

"No problem. When you text Karo about the money, put 'blueprint' after everything you say to her. She will know what that means and you can prepare for the next load."

Steve was excited. "So CeCe about to put together two semi trucks for me to buy. I already got two drivers that are set up with truck driver school and everything."

"Damn, you ain't messing around. I used to own a few semi trucks back in the day."

"I already got a contract for about $12,000 a week per truck so that should do it."

"That's good, nephew. I'm very proud of you. You've been making shit happen even though your surroundings have been wild. That speaks a lot about you." Swift nodded his head and smiled. He was truly proud of his nephew.

"Thank you. That means a lot coming from you. I'm really trying. It's just these girls that are my problem right now," he said, shaking his head.

"Well, one is in the hospital and the other one is on house arrest, so you should be okay for a minute with the headaches."

Steve laughed. "Hopefully . . . shit. Angelia ass is crazy as fuck."

"Well, she in trouble now, so maybe that will humble her a little and calm her down from doing all the silly shit. I don't get how she the one that cheated and she going straight crazy like you cheated on her. That don't make no damn sense."

"Right! That's what I'm saying."

"Most of them hood chicks out there ain't shit. I don't see how y'all can date them chicks, at all. It's a new breed nowadays. A woman used to hold a man down for real. I can't stand a liar myself, and that's what a lot of these girls seem to be lately. That shit like the ultimate red flag for me. You lie to me once, it's over, especially regarding some serious shit."

Steve was just listening thinking about all the times Angelia had lied to him. It definitely wasn't once. He couldn't even count how many lies he had caught her in over the years. "It's hard, and I feel what you saying, Unk. I just be trying to make it work versus starting over with another chick. Messing with this chick Shila though taught me some shit. We locked in with each other pretty fast, so I guess it's all about what you put into it, so to speak."

"That's true."

"I have to go back up to the hospital once I leave here. This shit is crazy. I can't believe Angelia did that shit. She is really tripping."

"Yeah, you better stay a clear distance from her. I hope you see that on your own now. She is not playing with you at all. She just caught herself a whole new case over you. That's what's silly to me. She did all this stupid shit, cheating, and now she ready to go to jail for life. She coulda killed that girl." Swift paused and looked Steve right in the eyes and continued, "She coulda killed you too. Don't forget that."

"Yeah, that is crazy."

CHAPTER
FORTY-TWO

Steve and his uncle sat and talked for a few more hours about all of Steve's plans. Steve discussed the changes he wanted to make as far as his cocaine organization went as well as the 'Angelia and Shila' situation. By the end, Steve sounded like he really knew how to handle everything with Angelia. He thanked his uncle for all the advice and left, excited to go up to the hospital to check on Shila. She had really been there for him when he was at his worst, so it was only right for him to be there for her now.

Steve walked out of the visiting room and he was hit with a cold breeze as he got outside. The wind gusts blew his shirt and cooled his body off quickly. It felt like the temperature had dropped twenty degrees over the last few hours he was in there. Steve walked quickly to his truck. He was so happy that his uncle was getting him all set back up with Karo, he went to pull out his phone to text Karo, and it started ringing. It was Shila's mom.

"Hello," Steve answered.

All Steve could hear was crying. "She . . . didn't make it," her mom said.

"What? Damn . . . I'm so sorry," he said and took a long pause as tears fell.

She sniffled, "It's okay. It's going to be okay, hunny. I'm fine, but you call me if you need anything, you hear me?"

"Yes, I hear you. I will," he said as his voice cracked.

"Okay, I'll be in touch," she said before hanging up. He had only met Shila's mom a few days ago, and she had been telling him how he needed to marry her daughter because Shila needed someone like him in her life. At first, they just met each other in passing, when they were taking shifts to keep Shila company, but eventually they started sitting with each other and talking for hours.

Steve was hurt over the whole thing. Tears fell down his face, but he tried to hold it all together even though a big part of him felt like this whole thing was his fault. He sat there in his truck for about 10 minutes, browsing through his phone, checking text messages, and responding to them. He sent James a text telling him Shila had passed away, but said he would call him later to talk more about it. He had several missed calls from Angelia calling from the county jail. Her lawyer had also called and left a voicemail. After he listened to it, Angelia was calling again. He accepted the charges for the call after the recorded operator voice went through.

"Hello," he said, calmly.

"Hey! What's taking so long? When y'all coming to get me?"

Steve paused. Her voice was filled with excitement, and he was sitting there dealing with Shila's death. "She's dead, Angelia. She's dead."

"Who?"

"Shila," Steve replied.

"How? I thought she was doing good and was going to make it."

"I don't know much about what happened. I just got a call saying she didn't make it."

Angelia's heart dropped and something came over her. The weight of her circumstances finally set in for her. "So what exactly does that mean for me?"

"The lawyer left a voicemail asking for more money now since you are going to be facing murder charges. Plus, he said it wouldn't be smart to go up for bond just yet. He said to give it a week or so."

"Oh, my God! This is crazy, Steve. I don't know what to do," she said as she broke down crying. She didn't want to say much over the recorded line, but she was in shock. She wished she could go back and undo what had been done. "Am I ever going to get out, Steve?"

"Yes, just hold tight. Let me see what's going on."

"Promise me, Steve. Promise me you going to do everything you can to get me out of here," she said as she cried nonstop.

Steve was beginning to cry again as well. This whole situation was terrible. "I promise."

He listened while Angelia cried through most of the phone call. Finally, the operator came on saying they had one minute left.

"I love you."

"I love you too," Steve responded, crying himself. "I'm going to get you out of there soon. I'll figure something out."

"Okay."

The phone call ended and Steve sat there for a minute before driving away. He drove straight to Shila's house because he knew how people were whenever someone died. He met James over there. James helped him go through his things, and gather it all up.

They drove to the hotel and Steve called CeCe to tell her to find something for him today, if possible. About two hours later she called him back.

"Hello. Tell me something good," Steve answered.

"Hey, Steve. So look, I found you two houses. Both of them are in Rochester and are only about three minutes away from each other."

"Rochester is nice. Give me some specs on the houses."

"Well, they are both nice houses. I'd take either one of them, no problem. Both of the homes are right around 3,500 square feet. One has 4 large bedrooms with 5 bathrooms, and the other one has 5 bedrooms with 4.5 baths and the master is on the main level. The subdivisions are pretty similar, and right down the road from each other. The 4 bedroom place is listed at $452,000, and the 5 bedroom is listed at $456,500. The lots are similar too. They are pretty nice sized half acre lots, so you'd have plenty of yard. And -."

Steve interrupted, "Sorry for cutting you off, but I'll take them both. These are both available for rent, right?"

"Oh, no problem. Yeah, you could rent either one."

"Okay, cool. Yeah, I'll take both of them. Can you hang on a quick second?"

"Yeah," CeCe replied.

Steve put the phone on mute and asked James if him and Eboni could go get the places for him today. James said they were free and would take care of it.

"Alright, CeCe. Sorry about that. My friend James and his wife Eboni will be calling you later to get everything taken care of for the houses. Just let them know what you need from them. I'ma give James your number if that's cool."

"Yeah, no problem."

They finished their conversation, and James went home to get Eboni. It took them a few days to get everything settled, but they made it happen.

CHAPTER **FORTY-THREE**

Over the next few days, Steve arranged for a load from Karo to be dropped off at the motel he bought. This time, he got 500 kilos of cocaine. Business was growing at a break neck speed, and most of Steve's time was spent managing it all. The rental car spot now had 20 cars with stash spots in them. Everyone was busy doing their part. Due to the quality, consistency, and price, nobody could touch what they were doing. There was no real competition. Everyone else was cutting their coke too much and being greedy, trying to charge too much. Business was running like a well oiled machine, and they were steadily making connections with new dope boys, putting them on the team to move more product. Steve had little time to think about the insanity of the last few months of his life. He was staying busy, and it was good for him mentally.

The funeral was coming up soon, and everyone on the streets was talking about how Angelia killed Shila. Angelia had gotten into two fights in one week with people that knew Shila. Shila knew a lot of people, and everyone around her was overwhelmed with grief due to her loss. Shila had so much going for her, and was a great mother. Everyone had a hard time believing she was really gone.

Steve woke up the following morning to his phone ringing. It was the lawyer. "Hello," he answered in a sleepy voice.

"Hi, Steve. I received the payment about two minutes ago. Thank you. Soooo . . . I'm thinking I can get her out on bond, but she will be on house arrest. With your last payment, my services are covered, but you will have to cover the cost of the bond. I can get her out as soon as today. Is she still going to be tethering at her parents' house?"

Steve had to think for a minute. He wasn't sure if he wanted her at his new house or not. Even though he knew she was nuts, he had missed her for some reason. "Damn, um . . . just do her parents' house. So she can't leave at all?"

"No, not at all. But in about six months we might be able to make some changes, if she does good of course."

"Okay, just do her parents' house then. That will be fine."

"You got it, Steve. Thanks, buddy. I'll get all this wrapped up and get her out of there in the next few hours. I already have the number to call for the bond." He paused for a few seconds. "Yep, I think that's everything. Cool. Talk to you soon, Steve."

"Okay, sounds good. Thanks."

Later that day, after Steve ran around picking up money, he took everything to his safe house. He used one of the new houses to lay his head at, and the other one as his safe house. Angelia had called him nonstop since she was released, and was telling him to come over. He made it over there at about 10 o'clock that night. He called her when he pulled up.

"Where are you?" she answered.

"Outside. Open the door," he told her as he parked on the street and went inside. She was so happy to see him.

"Papi!" she said, smiling then jumping and kissing him all over his face and lips. "I missed you so much! It was horrible in there. I do not want to go back there, ever. Jail is not for me."

Steve laughed as he followed her inside the house. They went down to the basement. It was a nice, finished basement that had light cream carpet floors, a full bathroom, and two bedrooms. "Where your parents at?" he asked when he got to the bottom of the stairs.

"They upstairs, asleep. I told them you was coming."

"This is nice," Steve said as he walked around, and opened the door to the room. It wasn't a big room, but it had a nice 3 piece bedroom set with a big TV mounted to the wall. "You got your little queen size bed, dresser with mirror, and a TV in here, I see you," he said, jokingly.

"Shut up!" She giggled. "I should be at your house."

"Naw, you like to burn shit down. I'm not about to keep throwing money out the window, playing with you. You think this shit a game for some reason."

She giggled again. "No, I don't."

"You do, but it's okay. I'm actually glad to see you," he said, sitting down on the bed. She climbed on top of him and straddled him.

"I'm happy to see you too."

"I know you miss me. I miss you too, but why did you do that? You really murdered that girl. You coulda hit me."

CHAPTER **FORTY-FOUR**

Angelia rolled over on the bed, and sat up against the headboard. Her eyes filled with tears as she said, "I didn't mean to do that, I swear."

"This shit is serious. Like serious, serious."

"I know, I know. Trust me, I know. I went through a lot of bullshit being locked up. I had to fight all these girls until they moved me. I swear I didn't want to actually kill her. She shot at me first. I didn't come at her like that at all."

"You smashed her car window out, then smashed your car into her. I know you didn't come at her with a gun at first, but damn."

"Damn, what?"

"This is some stressful shit. I'm trying to figure out how the hell you going to get out of this."

"Well, you got me a good lawyer. All I can do is pray at this point, Steve. I guess love makes you do crazy shit. In the moment when I was shooting, I was just shooting back to make her stop shooting before she hit me. I didn't even know I hit her. I was honestly not shooting to kill her when I did that."

"I know, I know. That's what bullets do though. Damn . . . Fuck!" he yelled. He was starting to really stress out about this whole thing again. And now that he was with Angelia in person, he realized he really did love her. "I wish I could just take the charge for you, damn."

"Come here," she said, opening her arms up wide and reaching for him while he still sat at the foot of the bed. He came to her, and she grabbed his face and kissed his lips softly. "Everything is going to be okay. God knows I didn't mean to do that." She kissed him again, then licked him from his chin up to his nose.

He backed up and wiped his face off. "Why you always doing that?" he smiled, laughing. "You so nasty," he joked.

She giggled. "I just like licking you, that's all. I thought you liked it when I licked you."

He smiled and pushed her away. "I'm playing. Yeah, I like it when you lick me. I love it."

"Okay, so why did you back up when I licked you then? Like you didn't want my tongue on you?"

"You just shocked me and caught me off guard. You ain't licked me like that in a long time."

She giggled. "Oh, yeah? Come here," she said as she used her index finger to signal him to her. When he got close she grabbed his face and licked him again from his nose to his eyebrow.

"What do I taste like? You always like to lick me in all these weird spots."

"You taste good and clean, just like I like it." She kissed him on the lips, peck after peck until he eventually laid on his back beside her. She put her arm around him and rested her head on his arm and looked up at him. He couldn't believe how fast she was able to turn his mood around. He also couldn't believe how quickly he immediately felt attached to her again, especially after all that had happened. Everything felt right to him at the moment, and he didn't want to change the mood, so he let her do whatever she was doing.

Before he knew it, she had his dick in her mouth and was sucking it like she wanted to swallow the whole thing. She sucked and licked all over his dick and balls, then moved back up to his stomach with her tongue. She nibbled on his pecks as she stimulated his nipples before making her way back down to his dick. "I want you to cum in my mouth," she said as she started sucking and stroking him nice and slowly. Steve didn't stop her. He let her continue until she had his toes curling as she was licking around his asshole.

"Damn, baby," he whispered, letting her know he loved what she was doing. She kept licking and kissing his asshole softly while stroking his dick. His legs were bent backward, which felt a little awkward to him, but made the sensation feel better. She kept licking, then made her way back up to his shaft, and started to suck again. About 40 seconds passed before his dick swelled up and exploded down her throat, where she had it buried at the moment. She kept it down her throat the whole time he came, and the feeling of it blew his mind.

"What the fuck," he moaned as he came down from his high.

"You liked that?" she asked as she sat up, and swallowed down the last bit of his cum.

"Hell yeah. I didn't know you could do that. You gonna get yo' ass beat."

They both laughed. "Shut up! I just be trying different stuff."

"Naw, fuck that. That wasn't no try. That was some pro shit."

She giggled as she shook her head. "Whatever, Steve."

"Now you lay on your back. It's my turn."

She happily did as he requested.

"Wait, I got something for you," he said as he dug in his pants pocket and grabbed a small baggy with some cocaine inside of it. As soon as she saw it, a big smile came across her face.

CHAPTER
FORTY-FIVE

"Oh yeah, Papi," she said, jumping to her feet and clearing off a spot on the dresser for him. They both snorted a few lines off the dresser. Within minutes, he pushed her on the bed, and dove between her legs. He aggressively ate her pussy nonstop for about 20 minutes, during which she had two explosive orgasms. After the second time she came, he flipped her over and ate her ass and pussy from the back while she was in a doggy style position. She came again after a few minutes, then he got up on his knees and put his dick inside of her. She moaned as he started stroking away. He was concerned about her being loud because her parents were upstairs, but she was acting like she didn't care at all. She was moaning and calling him Papi while he was stroking.

"You gotta be quiet, boo," he said quietly, hoping it would at least quiet her down a little.

She just laughed. "He can't hear me. Keep going, Papi."

"You sure?"

"Yessss. You think I ever want my dad to hear me having sex? No."

He laughed and went back to pounding away at her from behind. Her pussy soaked his dick as he looked down and watched it go in and out of her. Soon, he flipped her over, and got on top and put his dick deep inside her, while he tongue kissed her. She wrapped her legs around his waist and moaned. "Oh, my God. That feels so good, Papi. I miss you so much," she whispered. "It feels so good," she said, closing her eyes. He continued to kiss her passionately as they tried to swallow each other's tongues. Her legs locked him deep inside her, but he still had enough movement to press around her walls. "I'm going to cum, Papi. Don't stop," she whispered, twirling her hips under him. "Si, Papi, siiiii!" she said as her body began to tremble in an overpowering orgasm.

They had been at it for about an hour now, and the cocaine had him standing tall inside her. He was now laying sideways across the bed, and she was on her back with her head towards the headboard. He lifted her leg up and inserted his dick in her pussy slowly, before pumping away for about 15 minutes until he came inside her. Once he pulled out, she licked her pussy juices off his dick and laid on his chest. They were both covered in sweat and breathing heavily. "I love you so much, Papi."

"I love you too," he replied, looking in her eyes.

They fell asleep shortly after that. A few hours later, at about 3 in the morning, Angelia woke up and snorted another line off the dresser. She climbed back in bed, pulled Steve's dick out, and put it in her mouth, sucking it until it got hard and he woke up. Soon, she got on top of him and rode him until he came again, and they went back to sleep.

Steve's eyes didn't open again until about 10 o'clock that morning. The feeling of wet pussy on his face startled him awake. Angelia was riding his face when his eyes opened. He looked up at her and could tell that she had clearly been up doing coke all night. Her pussy was dripping all over his face, and he started to help her do what she was doing by sucking and licking on her. She came within a few minutes of him licking, then laid down next to him. His face was soaking wet. As Steve looked at her laying next to him, he noticed she looked tired and kind of strung out.

"I got you good," she said, wiping the wetness from his face.

"Horny ass! You just gone ride my face until I wake up, huh?" Steve laughed.

She giggled. "I had been trying to wake you up so I figured you would wake up once you tasted this pussy on your lips . . . and it worked!"

CHAPTER
FORTY-SIX

He laughed. "At first I thought I was getting suffocated, shit. Where's my phone? You seen it?"

"Nope. It was on the dresser."

He looked around on the bed and the dresser, but didn't see it. Eventually he found it right under the edge of the bed. He had 6 missed calls and a few text messages. The first message he opened was from James, reminding him that the funeral was today, and that he was going to ride with him. He glanced at the time, and realized he had overslept and had to leave right away if he was going to make it on time. "Fuck. I gotta go. I'm not even dressed. Damn, I didn't know my phone was on silent."

Angelia's face immediately scrunched up in anger. She knew the funeral was today, and she had put his phone on silent and hid it under the bed to prevent him from going.

"Where you going?" she asked with an attitude and a dirty look on her face.

"To the funeral," Steve said, putting on his shirt.

"The funeral?"

"Yeah, to pay my respect."

"Why the fuck would you go to a funeral for a bitch I killed over you?"

Steve was speechless. He stood there looking at her while he finished getting dressed. "What the fuck?" he finally said. "I went to school with her. This ain't someone I just met."

"Was she pregnant with your baby or just saying that to piss me off?"

"Angelia! Are you serious? Why you acting like this? She's dead. Why do it even matter?"

"Sooooo, that's a yes. You was fucking her. Yep, you was. Raw at that."

Steve shook his head, and grabbed the rest of his stuff to leave.

"Was you fucking her?" she screamed as she smacked him upside the back of his head.

He turned around and pushed her into the wall. "Keep yo' fucking hands to yourself, fo' I knock your ass out."

She slapped him hard across the face. "You ain't going to knock shit out!"

Steve grabbed her by the neck and started choking her. "What the fuck is wrong with you?" he said as he squeezed tighter and tighter. "Ain't nobody playing with you." She struggled to breathe, and pulled at his hands, trying to pry them loose. She tried scratching at him, but he was significantly stronger than her, and it only made him squeeze her neck tighter. Her whole face was purple and red looking, and she couldn't get in a single breath. He slammed her head back into the wall, then let her go. She dropped straight to the floor, and gasped for air.

"Now, quit playing with me."

She stood right back up and ran at him swinging. To avoid hitting her, he just curled up on the bed and let her hit him until she tired herself out. "You fucking crazy," he said as he took the hits over and over, hoping her parents didn't hear them fighting. Angelia was now screaming as she punched him.

"You not going to that fucking funeral!" she shouted, as she slammed her bedroom door shut.

"What the fuck is wrong with you?" Steve asked as he got up, trying to fix himself. Angelia was standing in front of the door with her arms crossed with a sour look on her face.

"Ain't nothing wrong with me," she spat. "You're not going to that bitch's funeral."

"I'm about to call your mom down here. You tripping. Get out the way, damn." He tried to move her, but she punched him in the nose, and blood started to run down over his lips.

"What the fuck? Are you serious?" he grabbed his nose and pinched it. He wanted to throw her through the wall, but he didn't want her dad to flip on him. He sat at the end of the bed holding his nose. "Get me some tissue."

"Fuck you."

"Damn, straight up? Did you do too much coke or something?"

She ran at him swinging again, and he curled up while pinching his nose. She just wouldn't stop hitting him. "You . . . not . . . going," she said in between each hit, until he finally picked her up and slammed her on the bed. The blood running from his nose got all over when he slammed her. Once she hit the bed, he took off running up the stairs and out the side door.

He was out of the house when he heard her scream, "Mutherfucker!" as she chased after him.

CHAPTER FORTY-SEVEN

Steve was almost to his truck when he looked back and saw Angelia coming out of the house with a baseball bat. He got inside his truck, but before he got it started, she had hit the windshield and the driver's side window. "Get the fuck out!" she yelled, now hitting the doors of the truck. Her dad heard the commotion and came walking out of the house. He saw his daughter beating the truck wildly and yelling.

"What's going on?" he asked as he walked across the grass. She continued to scream and hit his truck. "Angelia!" he yelled as he tried to stop her from hitting the truck any more. Angelia had drops of blood on her face and shirt, and he thought she was bleeding at first.

Steve stepped out of the truck and ran away from her. "She's crazy, man!" he yelled, pointing at her as she had the bat cocked back, ready for another swing.

"Come here, Steve. Right now!" she screamed as she chased him.

"Angelia!" her dad yelled again, trying to get her attention.

"Papi, he hit me! So now I'ma hit his ass back."

"She lying! I didn't hit her," Steve yelled as he tried to keep his distance from her.

"You hit my daughter?" her dad yelled, staring at Steve with a furious look on his face.

"She's lying!" Steve shouted, still making sure he stayed out of the way of the bat. He was regretting getting out of his truck.

"Angelia, get in the house! Your tether is going crazy!" her dad shouted.

"Tell him to come back inside, and I'll go inside!"

"Steve, I don't know what's going on, but will you please come back inside so she won't go to jail?"

"Tell her to put that bat down first!" he yelled as she took another swing at him with it.

"Give me the bat," her dad said calmly while holding out his hand.

Angelia gave her dad the bat and started walking toward the house. Steve took a few steps behind her like he was following behind, then turned and ran fast to his truck. He jumped in and sped off, burning rubber down the street. Within seconds, his phone was going off. It was Angelia. He ignored it and kept driving as quickly as he could directly back to the house. He called James on the way to tell him what happened and how crazy Angelia was.

"Why you keep going around that girl? You making her act crazy. She ain't allowed to leave the house, or she goes back to jail, and you go there? That don't make no sense, bro. Leave her alone."

"She just got out. I was just checking on her, making sure she was still good. She's my baby momma."

"Bro, it sound like you better leave her alone, before she kill your ass next. She's getting worse, even facing a murder trial she's acting crazy."

Steve laughed. "She den fucked the truck all up. She busted my windshield and my driver window. Her ass put dents all in the doors too. She was beating the fuck out the truck before she came at me."

"Man, fuck that truck. Make an insurance claim. I'm on my way to pick you up. Be ready when I get there. I ain't trying to be late to this funeral."

"I'll be ready. Come through," Steve said as he pulled up at his house and hung up the phone.

CHAPTER
FORTY-EIGHT

Text messages were coming in from Angelia.

Angelia: Stupid bitch! I hate you!

Angelia: You don't love me.

Angelia: Come back.

Angelia: Answer the phone!

He ignored all the messages, then she started calling as he got into the house. She called nonstop, back to back, until he eventually answered. "What!" he shouted.

"When you coming back?" she cried into the phone.

"Angelia, why are you crying?"

"I'm just going through a lot. I don't know what to do. I'm so stressed out, Steve. I can't believe you going to her funeral."

"You have to relax. You about to get yourself locked back up. You caused a whole scene over some real dumb shit. That girl is dead now. Got it? D-E-A-D, dead. Why didn't you tell me you was fucking her baby daddy?"

"Why would I tell you that?" she asked, getting an attitude.

"I'm talking about when I used to ask you about why you hated her so much."

"I don't remember you asking me that."

"Right before we got these tattoos on us, I asked you."

"What does this have to do with you going to her funeral?"

"Nothing. I was just asking." Steve had stripped his clothes off at this point and was standing in the bathroom. He had brought his suit and dress shirt into the bathroom on a hanger so he could get dressed as quickly as possible. He turned on the water then got into the shower with one airpod in his ear.

"What's that noise?"

"The shower," he said as he squeezed some body wash on his towel.

"Oh, so you really about to go to her funeral?"

"Yes, I am."

She started crying again. "Can you come back later please?"

Steve ignored her as he tried to quickly wash his body.

"Steve? Do you hear me? I asked if you can come back later. Please, Steve?"

"If you learn how to act, I'll come back. I'm not about to be dealing with you acting crazy and shit when I'm around."

"Okay . . . I won't. Sorry," she said, trying her best to sound apologetic.

"You always do crazy ass stuff, then you say sorry. While you were chasing me around with that bat, you lied right to your dad, talking about I hit you and you're trying to get your hit back, like we're kids. You really outside clowning and acting a fool and you already in real trouble, for murder at that. Do you not care about life? On top of all that, you know everything I have going on right now, and you keep tempting me on so many levels."

"I'm sorry, Steve. I told my dad that I lied about you hitting me and I only said it because I was mad. I'm just stressed Steve and I don't know what to do. I feel like I'm losing everything, including you. You not paying me as much attention as you were before. It's like the only reason you still dealing with me is because I have your baby. My life is just falling apart on every single level. This shit is not fair at all. I may go to jail for the rest of my life over something I did out of love." Steve listened to her as she cried while he was rinsing off his body. He did feel bad for her, but he wanted her to see how she was acting. "I'm not built for no jail shit," she cried even more.

"It's going to be okay. You have one of the top lawyers in Michigan. Just try to stop thinking about the worst case scenario."

Steve climbed out of the shower and started to dry himself off and get ready. "Think positive and try not to think about the future. You've gotta stay in the now. If you spend all your time worrying about what you coulda done different, you just beating yourself up. So, like I said, stay in the now . . . in the present . . . right now, you good. You got a good lawyer, a supporting family, and I'm looking out for you. You out on bond instead of sitting in a jail cell. You keep thinking about all the possible bad outcomes and you will drive yourself crazy, and start acting crazy like you did earlier. So just chill. Everything is going to be okay."

She was still crying. After a few seconds she responded, "I know."

"Oh, and another thing . . . I'm not ever doing that shit with you anymore. You was up doing that shit all damn night. I seen you getting up and doing lines. That's probably why your ass was acting all crazy like that. You didn't sleep at all, plus you was high as hell. So that's it for me. After seeing that shit, I'm done. I'm not doing that again with you."

"Okay," she sniffled.

Steve sprayed cologne on his neck and checked himself out in the mirror. He was ready to go once he put on his suit jacket and tie. "I'll call you later and see what you up to. Tell your dad to call me too. That was disrespectful as hell to your parents, making a big scene outside in front of the neighbors and all that. So have him call me in a few hours so I can talk to him."

"Okay," she sniffled.

"Bye."

CHAPTER
FORTY-NINE

Steve tied his tie then opened up the bathroom door. "Damn, nigga!" Steve yelled, surprised to see James in his room. "You scared the shit outta me."

They both laughed. "My bad. I knocked for a while. You ain't answer so I came in. I figured you was probably in the shower."

Steve looked down at James' suit and back up at him. "Shit, you clean up alright." Both of them had on all black high end designer suits. They both wore a crisp, white dress shirt and a black silk tie. They looked clean, classic, and tailored. Their fresh hair cuts and line ups topped everything off perfectly.

They left through the garage of Steve's house to head to the funeral. James brought his new, black S550 Benz, which he had looking like a black sheet of glass. The sun was bright and there wasn't a single cloud in the sky. They didn't say much on the way there. James turned on the radio, and they just chilled most of the way. When they got close they saw it was packed. The street was blocked off and people were parking way down the street and walking up to the funeral home. As they drove to where they could find a spot, they noticed a few people that they hadn't seen since high school. A few of the girls they remembered from back in the day were looking gorgeous in their dresses and heels. Some of the guys that were skinny in high school were now bulked up and muscular. Some of the former football players were looking fat and out of shape. Everybody was looking different.

They walked inside the funeral home, greeting a few friends on the way in. James and Steve walked in together, and got in line to go pay their respects. The room was quiet, with only a few whispers heard from people sitting in the seats. As they got close to the body, Steve started to really feel that Shila was now gone. The loss of her was setting in as he was next in line and saw her in the casket. He looked at her and could see where they had covered up the bullet wound on her neck. They had done a very nice job on her hair and makeup, but that didn't take away from the fact that her spirit was no longer in her. The woman that motivated Steve to get into the trucking business, the woman that always tried to push him in a positive direction, was now gone.

Steve kneeled down and started praying. He started remembering some of the fun times they had together. He thought about her helping him up the stairs when he was a drunken mess, and her massaging his sore muscles in the hot tub. He thanked God for allowing them to experience that together.

He then stood up and looked at her one last time, and he placed his hand on her and quietly said, "Thank you." He walked away with his eyes filled with water as he fought back the tears. James stood there for a moment before meeting back up with Steve, and they found a spot along the back wall to stand. The service was very sad, and everyone was sobbing uncontrollably. Ace was sitting up front with Shila's children, who were not taking it well at all.

After the service, people crowded around outside and were sharing memories of Shila. As Steve and James walked out, they noticed a few people looking at them funny. Everybody knew what had happened, and Steve didn't really feel comfortable standing there. When he saw Ace outside, it didn't sit right with him at all. He wanted to fight him, but knew that this wasn't the time or place.

Steve walked up to Shila's mom, and noticed that a lot of people weren't too happy to see him. So after offering his apologies to her mom, he decided he was done, and they started walking back to James' car. Steve noticed someone looking at him.

"Hey, you," she said with a cheerful voice.

Steve smiled. "Hey, how are you? Wow, you still are beautiful, I see."

She blushed and smiled. "Thank you. You still handsome as well."

"What's up, Aliyah? How you doing?" James asked, noticing both of their eyes lighting up.

"I'm well. How are you?"

"Can't complain."

"Where you on your way to? You want to grab some food or something?" Steve asked.

"Sure."

"Did you come alone?"

"Yes."

"Mind if I ride with you? I didn't drive."

"Yes, of course, come on."

"Oh, so y'all just going to leave me, huh?" James said, joking.

They all laughed. "Naw, you can come," Aliyah said.

"I'm kidding. Y'all go ahead. I'm just playing around."

Steve walked with Aliyah toward her car. "I finally caught up with you," she said.

"You said that like you been looking for me."

"I mean, I did tell you to give me a call, which you never did. But I see you been busy. You got all these girls going crazy for you out here."

"Yeah, it's been crazy lately. I had to get another phone and all kinds of stuff. I'm going to program your number back in now," he said as he climbed in her car and took out his phone. Steve looked around at the interior. "Damn, you're riding in the Tesla, huh? I see you."

She giggled. "Yes, I love this car."

He programmed her number in his phone. "Okay, I got you now."

"What kind of music you listen to?" she asked as she backed her car out of the parking spot. Steve looked at her as she put the car in drive. She was still so pretty.

"Anything really. I'll listen to whatever. It don't matter with me."

CHAPTER **FIFTY**

She put some music on, and Steve's phone vibrated. It was a text from James.

James: Damn, nigga. That's the one you supposed to be with right there. She is badd.

Steve: Lol you never know.

James: You better get her, bro.

Steve: We will see. You silly as hell.

"So, what you have a taste for?" Aliyah asked him as she turned down the music.

"Anything. I don't care."

"Okay, I have a place, no worries. You like sea food, right?"

"Yes, for sure. I love sea food."

"Okay, good. I'll take you to one of my favorite spots. I bet not see you in there with nobody after I take you there though, okay?"

He laughed. "You won't. If it's good, it will be our spot."

She giggled and turned the music back up. Aliyah drove to a restaurant in downtown Detroit that Steve had never been to before. They walked in together, and were seated at a nice table in the back that was covered in a clean, white tablecloth. The restaurant was known for its seafood, and had recently been visited by several food critics that gave it great reviews. The two of them looked classy and clean, sitting down at the table, and people were staring. She guided Steve on some of her favorite things on the menu. When the food came, it smelled fantastic, and they sat there for hours, drinking wine and laughing. She caught him all up on her life. She told him about her boyfriend, and how they barely had sex and that she had caught him cheating several times. Steve could relate, and he shared the similarities with his situation. Aliyah had remembered Angelia from high school, and wasn't surprised about how sneaky she was, but she kept her thoughts about her to herself out of respect for Steve. Steve could tell that Aliyah was a smart, solid girl with a good head on her shoulders. She wasn't the type that would go behind her boyfriend's back and cheat no matter how he treated her.

Steve smiled at her as they brought another glass of wine for each of them. "So, are you like completely done with him, or y'all still live together or doing whatever it is y'all doing?"

"No, I'm done with him now. He took me through a lot and I just sat there like a dummy and took it. I kept giving him chances, and he kept doing the same nonsense to me, so I'm all done. He's driving a car that I got him in my name, but I'm trying to get that back too. And once I do, I'm done with him for good."

"What you going to do with the car when you get it back from him?"

"I guess drive it and keep making the payments on it. As long as he don't have it, I'm happy. Why? You looking for a new car?"

"Maybe. What kinda car is it?"

“It's a Maserati Quattroporte Gransport, 4 door."

"Aww, hell naw! You doing it too big over there for me."

She giggled. "Whatever. You'd look so cute in it. It's midnight blue with a peanut butter interior," she said, laughing and knowing that Steve would love the car if he saw it. Juice had already told Aliyah a little bit about Steve. She knew she had to be outgoing to make sure he knew she liked him.

He was laughing at her sales pitch for the car. He took a sip of his wine then asked, "How much you owe on it?"

"It's a lease. I got about a year and a half left on it."

"Oh, okay. That ain't bad. How you know I'm responsible enough to handle a car like that?"

She giggled. "Come on now. Juice is like my big brother. And he loves your butt. He always speaks so highly of you. I'm always over there and we always plotting, trying to see how we can get you to come and chill, but you're always so busy. I just wanted to be around you and see how much you had grown since high school."

He laughed. "Wow! Really? So have I grown, at least a little bit?"

She giggled. "You've grown a lot! Besides this accident you just had, I think you're doing great. That situation threw me off, but everyone knows they were beefing over Shila's baby daddy. They had fought a few times while she was still with you. Everyone was talking about how you were being faithful to her even with what she was doing to you. I'm like, he must not really know what's going on with his girl."

"Naw, I didn't know. I'm just finding out all this stuff. She had videos with this guy and all that."

Aliyah shook her head. "Yeah, that's what I heard. I heard they was fighting this time because Shila gave you the videos of her and Ace or something."

"Yeah, basically. She had just been doing too much and I never knew. I was always working and trying to build a good future for us. I never cheated on her all the time we was together until the incident recently. That's when me and Shila started getting closer. And now look what den happened. This shit has been so crazy for me. I can't stop thinking about it."

"Yeah, that's messed up. We both den got messed over. It's cool though, that's just God telling us that there is something greater out there for us."

Steve nodded. "Facts."

CHAPTER
FIFTY-ONE

"You want another drink? By the way, this meal on me," she told him, smiling.

"No, not even. I'm not letting that happen today."

"Oh, you one of them, huh? The man must always pay, type of guy?"

"I mean . . . "

"Yep."

He busted out laughing. "The man should pay, I feel."

"It don't always have to be like that though. I like going back and forth. You can take care of it next time, if you want a next time, that is," she said as she smiled at him.

"Oh, there will be. And thank you for the meal. So you want another drink?"

"Sure." Aliyah ordered two more drinks for them, and they continued to talk and laugh. Neither of them wanted to leave. Steve was like a breath of fresh air for her. He was very focused in on her and everything she was saying. He could tell that she was really interested in him also. She could tell that he was different, but she wanted to make sure because it was so rare for a man to be with just one girl. She wanted this to be real. She hadn't dated in a long time, but Juice had been trying to talk to her about Steve for awhile now, and she finally had him in front of her, in the flesh.

"I still can't believe you didn't know about Angelia. Like, you live in Pontiac . . . How did you miss that? Pontiac is so small, and all they do is run they mouth."

He laughed. "People was saying stuff, but I didn't believe it. I never noticed it in her behavior or nothing. I just didn't want to accuse her of something that I didn't have any proof of."

"But when multiple people kept telling you the same stuff, didn't that make you think there could be something to it? I mean, that would raise an eyebrow for me."

"I feel you, but I was busy working. I thought me and her was on the same page, honestly."

"I'ma need you to not be that naive again. Or even deal with a chick like that again. You're better than that, Steve."

"Well, I'm stuck with her for the next 18 years. She's pregnant."

"It's okay. What's done is done. So it is what it is. I would like to date you, but not if you are still wanting to have sex with her. I know you would have to deal with her because you'd be the father of her kid. But that girl is crazy, and I don't want any problems. These girls out here killing over dick now," she said, shaking her head.

"That's understandable. I want to date you too, and I don't have a problem cutting her off or whatever."

Aliyah nodded and finished her glass of wine, and Steve went on saying, "If me and you was ever to get serious, I promise I'd never be having sex with her and then coming home and having sex with you. It sounds like both of us already dealt with that, and I wouldn't want that happening to me again, so I would never do that to you."

"I would hope not," Aliyah said with a smile.

"I won't for sure. That ain't what I do. I'm the type of guy that's okay with sleeping with one woman. I don't need a whole bunch of girls. I was never like that, you know that. Even in high school, I always had a girlfriend and was always faithful."

"You sure did. I used to be like, he always got a girlfriend and I'm never going to get a chance with him," she said, giggling.

He laughed. "You funny. I didn't think you even looked at me like that."

"I did. I was just shy back then, that's all."

"That makes sense."

Aliyah noticed that Steve started to seem distracted. He kept glancing down at his phone. Angelia was calling and sending him text messages over and over again.

CHAPTER **FIFTY-TWO**

Angelia: Damn, you fucking that bitch too?

Angelia: Answer the phone.

Angelia: Why you leave with Aliyah? Where y'all going?

Angelia: Are you fucking her now?

Angelia: Pick up the phone! You just going to keep sending me to voicemail? OK!

Aliyah smiled at Steve and said, "So you a busy man, huh? Do your phone always be jumping like that?"

"No, not at all. This the same person calling over and over."

"Angelia?"

"Yes. She is nuts. I'm trying to be nice since she's out on bond and can't go nowhere, but she going to mess that up in a minute. She really out her damn mind," Steve said as he shook his head and placed his phone face down on the table so he would stop seeing the notifications. He started looking around.

"She will be alright," Aliyah said, flagging down the waitress and signaling for her to bring them both another glass of wine.

"She gonna have to be. So what else you been doing other than houses and stuff?"

"I mainly be into crypto currency."

"I don't know much about crypto. I heard of it, but I hear people always talking like it's a scam or something."

She giggled. "No, it's not a scam, at all. People are silly for judging something without doing their own homework. I mean, if you gonna say something about a topic, at least do your research before you go talking like you know something about it, ya know? Crypto is basically digital currency. It's not all that much different than paper money. It's just the direction the world is headed, so I'm not going to resist the direction the world is going. There's no point to. I'm definitely going to have to give you some lessons on it to bring you up to speed. But before I forget, Juice told me to tell you about a deal that came across my desk last week. I just never called you, but there are ten houses, all on the same block. They aren't right next to each other, but they are close. Well, a few of them are right next door, but not all of them. They only want $250,000 for all of them, and a few of the houses are worth $60-70,000 individually. They are all in Pontiac, but the home values in Pontiac are going up. An old white couple owns them. The lady's husband just died. She's like 85 years old and is itching to get rid of them."

"Damn. Are there any liens or is anything owed on them?"

"No back taxes, no liens, or anything on them. They are all free and clear. I was trying to come up with the money myself, but I ain't looking too good at the moment. I'm tied up in a few other things. I told her I'd give her $20,000 down and pay her off in a couple years, but she wants the whole $250,000 so she can just be done with it."

Steve was nodding his head while she was telling him about them. It sounded like a good deal to him. "So, how much can you come up with then?" he asked.

"Maybe about thirty thousand, but that's everything I have saved that's liquid right now."

"I'm trying to see how we can go 50/50 on them." Steve took a drink of his newly delivered glass of wine.

"Loan me $125,000 and you pay the other $125,000. Then we split everything down the middle. There are already tenants in all of the homes."

"Damn, for real? How's the payment history for the current tenants?"

"Solid. She said all of them been in the houses for more than three years. She has two of them that have been in there for more than five years, so we don't have to worry about that. We will walk in and start making our money back right away."

"Yeah, let's do that. I'm down."

"How soon can you get the money into my account?"

CHAPTER
FIFTY-THREE

"Shit, I can have it done right now. You have your account number, routing number, and all that on hand? I'll get it wired right now."

She giggled. "Oh, you serious, serious. I like that. Yes, I have my account info," she said, smiling at him. She had believed everything he had said, but it was still hard to believe that he could send that kind of money right then and there. "Here you go," she said as she placed her phone up on the table in front of him with the account numbers. He picked up his phone and called John, telling him what he needed him to do. John got on it right away. Five minutes later, she checked her account, and it showed $250,000 pending.

"Oh, shit," she said with big eyes, looking up at him, then her phone.

"What?"

"It's pending."

"You look surprised," he said with a smirk.

She giggled. "I mean, I am. Damn. So many people playing out here. Wait, this isn't a scam or nothing is it? I'm not going to get in trouble, am I?"

He laughed. "Naw, I'm legit. You see where it's coming from. That's a legit business. Do we got a deal or what?"

She smiled. "Hell yeah," she said, standing up and walking around the table with her arms out for a hug. "Oh, my God. I'm so excited!" she said in a high-pitched, squeaky voice. "Thank you so much for this. I'm going to pay you back everything with interest. I'm so glad we could jump on a deal like this."

He laughed and felt chills through his body due to the excitement he saw in her. It always made him happy to make other people happy. "You welcome. And thank you back. Shit, that is a good deal on those houses."

"But you still didn't have to put me in like that and you did, so thank you. I really appreciate that. God is so good."

"No problem. No worries, I'm rocking with you. Let me know what other good deals you find out there." Steve trusted her just based on Juice's word alone. He was solid and they never had a single issue. On top of that, Juice told him that Aliyah made good money all on her own, so he wasn't worried about it.

"I'm so happy," she said, as she sat back down. She couldn't stop smiling. She lifted her glass. He clinked his glass against hers and they both took a sip. She then gave him a big, beaming smile that revealed her beautiful, white teeth.

"You're so cute. I'm loving your little smile over there."

She started blushing hard, her face was beet red. "Thank you. You are too much of a sweetheart."

"That's a bad thing?"

"Not when you dealing with a woman like me, it's not. But for some women, that would be a bad thing. A lot of girls like guys that don't treat them well, but that's not me. I love a respectful gentleman who is in tune with his emotions and all that. I find that so sexy." She smiled and took another drink. She wanted to learn more about Steve. She was so impressed by how he had matured since high school, and he was backing up what he had to say with action. Aliyah got up and excused herself to go to the bathroom. She was curvy and all natural. Steve loved the way her butt jiggled a little differently while she walked away. He looked down at his phone and frowned. It was filled with a bunch more nonsense from Angelia. He made sure to put his phone away by the time Aliyah came back.

CHAPTER **FIFTY-FOUR**

About an hour later, Aliyah dropped Steve off at James' house. Before he got out of the car, they pecked on the lips a few times, and both told each other that they were looking forward to seeing one another soon. Steve got out of the car and watched her drive away. He was already infatuated with her, and he had had a great time with her.

When he walked into the house, he was smiling from ear to ear. "Damn, bro. She got you smiling like that?"

"Yes, sir. This girl is amazing. I'm feeling her for sure! Angelia's crazy ass needs to get some help. She called and texted like a hundred times. I know she ain't got shit to do in the house all day, but damn. She's threatening me and all types of shit. She's over there losing her mind, bro."

"Leave her ass alone. I don't know why you keep fucking with her. It's beyond ridiculous, bro."

"That's my baby momma. Plus, she going through a crazy situation right now. I at least gotta be there for her."

"Stop fucking her though," James said, staring at him.

"Shit, I can't," Steve said as he laughed.

"Well, I hope you don't mess up this situation with Aliyah because of Angelia. Angelia already showed you how she is. Aliyah is a good girl who is way out of Angelia's league. She got it going on, bro."

"Nigga, I just gave her $250,000 for ten houses. We locked in," Steve said, laughing.

"Damn, you loaned it to her?"

"Well, not really. We went into business together on ten houses with tenants already in them. I haven't seen what they look like just yet, but she gone show them to me soon."

"Oh, shit. That's dope. I forgot she is a real estate agent or broker or something like that. I remember Juice telling me about her a few times because that's where he gets all his houses. I was trying to work on something to get her and my wife to link up, but Eboni already had too much going on with what she was doing. You got your hands on a good one over there for sure. Be smart, bro. I never even heard niggas out there slandering her name about fucking niggas. Shit, I heard she ain't even give most niggas the time of day."

"Yeah, me neither. She been with the same dude forever. I need a chick like her on my team. Shila was on her shit like that too, but I wasn't really feeling her like that. I mean, I liked her and the pussy was good, but I think the kids and two baby daddy's threw me off. Now Aliyah, I'm feeling her for sure. She conducts herself like a woman and I'm getting a good vibe from her. She's got that good energy. She is so sweet too," Steve said, smiling.

"Shut yo' soft ass up. She so sweet," he said, mocking him and they both started laughing.

"Naw, bro. I can tell you are into her for sure. Just really think about how you move out here when it comes to Angelia. Don't mess up a good thing before it even gets started."

Steve looked down at his phone. "Man! This bitch still blowing my shit up. Let me step out and take this," he said as he walked out the side door. "What's up?"

"You ain't shit! You still with that bitch?"

"No. What the hell is wrong with you?"

"You not answering the phone for me and not responding to my texts, that's what's wrong with me. You acting funny now!"

"Acting funny about what?"

"Because your bitch dead!"

"Man, I will call you back. I'll be there later on," he said, then hung up the phone. She texted him right away calling him a bitch and he just shook his head and walked back inside. "Bro, this bitch is crazy. I don't know what happened, but she's completely lost her shit."

James laughed. "The pressure. She's under a lot of pressure. She just caught a murder case, you caught her cheating, caught her on video with another nigga, and you about to leave her ass. The nigga she was fucking with got killed. She's just going through it and spazzing out."

Steve hadn't thought of it like that. He had been so mad at her. "Yeah, you probably right. She's still out of her damn mind though."

They both laughed.

"Who's going to be normal with all that going on? Shit, I'd probably be snapping too," James said, still laughing.

CHAPTER **FIFTY-FIVE**

James drove Steve over to the rental spot, and he jumped into a car he had there with money in it. He had to run a few errands. First, he went by his cousins' house to make sure they had been going to the truck driving classes like they were supposed to. He was happy to hear that they hadn't missed a single class, and they had been actually enjoying it. They were almost done with the classes and were excited to start driving. He sat and talked with them for a few minutes before he left to drive to Angelia's house. He called Aliyah on the way.

"Hey!" she answered.

"What you doing?"

"Nothing. I was just cleaning up a little bit around the house. I'm going to write up a nice contract for us. That way everything is documented like it's supposed to be." Aliyah had a huge smile on her face as she walked around her kitchen. She was so happy that Steve had called.

"Okay, that's cool. I'm glad you know how to do contracts like that. That's a good skill to have for sure. I was calling becau-."

"Because you missed me?" she asked, jokingly cutting him off.

He laughed. "Yes, I miss you and becau-."

"Because you want to see me tomorrow?" she asked with a big smile.

"Dang, you got me again. Yes, I would love to see you tomorrow. You are too funny."

She giggled and started blushing. "That's you, playing right into it."

"You read my mind."

They both laughed.

"Naw, you forgot to tell me a little bit about crypto currency. You brought it up and I think we started talking about something else and then I forgot to come back to the topic. But you like the third person I heard talking seriously about it."

"Oh, yeah. Well, I know a little something about it. We can sit down and go through it in detail. It's not really much to it. For example, Bitcoin . . . you heard of that, right?"

"Yep."

"So, Bitcoin came out in 2009, right after the recession in 2008, I think it was. Yeah, that last recession where the housing bubble popped was in 2008. Well, after the market crashed, all those houses were dirt cheap. People that got into the housing market then made a killing."

"Right, right. So how does Bitcoin work? Like, where did this Bitcoin come from?" He laughed. "Is that a silly question?"

"Noooo, not at all. That's a common question that a lot of people have, believe it or not. So many people are scared of it because they don't understand it."

"Yeah, I've heard so many people saying it was a scam or that it's just for drug dealers and all that."

"See, that's what the banks want you to believe so you can stay away from it and keep using their system. You see, the banks are in trouble, and crypto currency and this blockchain is a huge threat to them. I'm talking so huge that it could literally cause a World War III."

"Damn, why is that?"

"When you transfer money, who do you use?"

"A bank?"

"Correct. With Bitcoin, when you send someone money, you are doing it through a system called blockchain, which is peer to peer. There is no middle man involved making money. So, basically, the bank isn't getting their cut, and it obviously upsets them. They aren't making easy money the way they used to, so they are trying to ban it in certain countries and talk negatively about it, referring to it as 'Fake Money' and stuff like that, just trying to discredit it. They want the control, you know? They want to be able to see what's going on like they have been doing for years. On top of that, they want to find a way to tax it, which has been a challenge for them as well."

"And what is blockchain?"

CHAPTER
FIFTY-SIX

"It's a technology that's a clear game changer. It allows for peer to peer transactions. You know when you send an email from your Yahoo or Gmail, or whatever you have?"

"Yeah."

"So, Yahoo, or whatever email provider you are using is essentially the middle man. That means they can see all your emails, including the ones you think are private. If Yahoo decides to shut down their company, you could theoretically lose your whole email address that you've had for years. Plus, you lose all of your emails. With the blockchain you get an address that's about 26-35 characters long. You don't have to remember it at all. You can put it into a QR code as well, and scan it with your phone. Blockchain is decentralized, which means there is no one person or group in control of it. Everyone that uses it is in control. And the only way for you to get scammed, hacked or whatever would be if 51% or more of the blockchain network agrees with it. There is a slim to none chance that would ever happen, so it's incredibly safe."

"So that's the only way it can get hacked?"

"Yep."

"So who came up with this Bitcoin, crypto shit? It doesn't sound like something a normal person would just be walking around thinking about."

She giggled. "Supposedly a person by the name of Satoshi Nakonto. But no one knows this person or even knows if he's a real person."

He laughed. "Oh, wow. Some weird shit, huh?"

"Yeah, kind of."

They both laughed. "So how can I make money with crypto?"

"Well, that's where I come in at. I study crypto all the time. I keep my eyes on the markets, so I watch it go up and down. I can tell you which ones to get and when."

"How many of them are there?"

"There are a lot right now, and new ones are being created every day. I just stick to the top 20 big ones."

"Okay, okay. Well, let me know when a big one is about to pop, and I'll dive in to see what happens."

"Okay, yeah, hold tight for now. I have my eye on a few of them and I'll let you know the right time to get in."

"So where do I buy it?"

"There are a lot of different places, but I tend to use Coinbase or Crypto.com."

Steve had now made it to Angelia's house, and was sitting in his car in the street talking to Aliyah for almost an hour. He had sent John a text message asking him if he knew anything about crypto. John sure did, and told him to let him know if he wanted to invest in it. John maintained several big accounts strictly for crypto investing, and he had them for years.

After he finally got off the phone with Aliyah, he walked up, and Angelia was waiting for him at the door. When he went inside, she just looked at him with her arms folded like she wanted to say something. Steve could tell she already had an attitude, but she was looking sexy.

"Damn, what's wrong with you?" Steve asked, already prepared for her bullshit.

"You," she responded.

"What did I do now?" he asked as he followed her down the stairs to the basement. When he got to the bottom of the steps he noticed a large number of small boxes stacked alongside the wall. "What's all this?" he asked, examining one of the boxes.

"My dad's favorite peanuts. He buys them in bulk."

Steve laughed. "I guess so. Damn, why he get so many though?"

Angelia giggled. "I told you, they're his favorites. I guess he just really likes them."

Steve ripped open one of the boxes and took a pack of the peanuts out. "I like peanuts too. I need to try these." Steve looked at the package for a second.

"My dad is going to kill you for opening that box."

"He will be alright," Steve said as he was reading the label. He opened up the bag and popped a couple of them into his mouth.

"Damn, these bitches fire!"

She giggled. "Now you see why he has so many."

"It all makes sense now," he said, devouring more of the peanuts. As he ate them, he looked Angelia up and down. She was looking sexy, wearing some baby blue spandex shorts that hugged her ass cheeks with a tight tank top. "Damn, that ass be looking fat," he said as he licked his lips. He watched her walk into her bedroom and start to do something at her dresser. He followed her in there, and she bent down to sniff up two lines of coke. "Where did that come from?"

"What?" she said, sniffing, and turning around to look at him.

"That coke."

"Oh, the coke." She laughed. "My dad. They was gone earlier so I snuck into his room and found his stash. I just got a lil' bit," she lied. Ace had been by earlier to drop it off to her.

Steve nodded. "I was just thinking . . . you're pregnant. You really need to stop doing that shit before my baby comes out all fucked up missing fingers or toes or something."

Angelia busted out laughing. "No, it's not going to come out like that. But, okay, I see your point. It probably isn't the smartest thing to do, so I'll stop after today. Sorry, I didn't really think about that. We gone have a baaaaaabyyyyyy," she said, smiling and walking toward him. She gave him a hug, then took a step back and said, "Anyways, where have you been?"

Steve smiled. "Why? You miss me or something?"

"I want to cut your dick off."

"Damn! Savage, huh?" he said as he pulled her close and kissed her on the lips. "Well, I missed you."

He grabbed her ass and squeezed it a little before giving it a smack. She grabbed his face and started kissing him. Her eyes began to drip and the tears flowed down her face.

CHAPTER
FIFTY-SEVEN

Steve backed his face up a little and looked at her. "Why you crying?" he asked.

"Just kiss me, please," she replied. They kissed aggressively and fell back on the bed. She started stripping his clothes off quickly while she kissed and bit his chest. Steve could tell that she was high as a kite. She was acting like an animal, but was crying at the same time, which confused him. She had his clothes off pretty fast, and his dick was in her mouth. She started sucking him like she was never going to see his dick again. He got hard quickly, and she looked up at his eyes as she stroked and sucked him. Tears kept falling from her eyes, and she took her lips off his dick for a second to say, "I love you so much, Papi." She went back to working his dick nice and slowly.

"I love you too," he said. She climbed on top of him and put his dick inside her slowly. She was soaking wet, and let out a quiet moan as he filled up her insides. She looked at him in his eyes and worked his dick slowly in a circle. She was twirling her hips around while pulling her ass cheeks apart with her hands to make his dick go inside deeper.

"This dick feels so good, Papi," she moaned as she continued to grind on him. She was acting like she was on ecstasy, the way she was into the sex. She started to move her hips faster and faster and eventually whispered, "I'm going to cum all over this dick." She licked his earlobe as she bounced her ass nonstop, up and down until she felt herself start to cum. "Oh, my God. I love you so much," she moaned as her body shook. She turned around, got on her hands and knees and arched her back and looked back at him. "Put it in my ass, Papi."

Steve licked all over her pussy and asshole from the back while she struggled to stay quiet. He got up then eased his dick inside her tight, wet asshole. "Fuck it hard, Papi! Fuck it hard, please," she moaned.

Steve started ramming her asshole, stroking in and out while she yelled his name with her face in a pillow to suppress the sound. "Papi!" she repeated again and again. Steve could barely make out the muffled words she was saying. He kept pounding away at her until her asshole felt like a wet pussy. He worked her until she started to tap out and run away from him, flipping over on her back breathing heavily. "Okay, okay, Papi. Damn!" she moaned while sweat covered her face. He soon slid back inside her asshole, and stroked her softly until he felt the pressure build up. He pushed his dick in as deep as he could while it began to pulse, and soon he was cumming inside her. "Papiiii," she whined. "That nut was supposed to go inside me for the baby."

He laughed, but her comment kind of weirded him out. He was breathing hard as he replied, "I got some more for you later, no worries."

After they were done, Angelia took him by the hand and walked him to a stand up shower that was part of the full bathroom in the basement. She turned on the water, and it got hot pretty quickly, so they stepped in together and washed each other's bodies off. She went to kiss him on the lips as the shampoo ran down his face.

"Pfffft! You all soapy," she said as she laughed, spitting the soap out of her mouth. The shower felt good to them, but they didn't stay in there too long. After they got out and dried off, they both went back to her bedroom and laid down on the bed naked.

Steve was on his back staring at the ceiling. Angelia looked at him for a few minutes before she spoke. "So, do you like her?"

"Like who?"

"Aliyah. Are y'all like trying to talk or what's going on? Why were you out eating with her?"

"We was talking business. Relax. I'm trying to buy some houses and shit. She knows a few rental properties that would be good for me. She's into real estate and knows a lot about it."

"I hear she was all blushing and everything."

"Damn, who told you that?"

"I got my sources," she said as she laid her head on his chest, and wrapped her fingers around his dick. "Who car is that outside?"

"That's a rental."

"You didn't have to get a rental. You can drive mines if you want to. It's just parked and I ain't allowed to go anywhere."

Steve laughed. "Naw, your ass will really be blowing me up then. If I had your car, you'd really be acting crazy. I ain't fucking with your car."

She giggled, and slapped him on the chest. "Whatever."

CHAPTER
FIFTY-EIGHT

As the weeks past, Steve was spending more and more time with Aliyah. She had taken him to see all of the rental properties they had purchased. The contract between them was signed, and the deal was done. Steve was really taken by her, and everything about her made him happy. She was fun, sexy, and drama free. They were seeing each other at least twice a day over the last month. Though they had yet to spend a night together, they were always holding hands and kissing when they would go out in public. They would go to the mall just to walk around and eat ice cream. A few of Angelia's friends saw them walking around the mall one day, holding hands, and they let Angelia know. That gave Angelia a clue as to why Steve had been missing a lot of her calls, and taking a long time to text back. She was pissed and wanted to get revenge so bad. She hated Aliyah with a passion, and her hatred was starting to overflow to Steve as well. She would be just nice enough for him to come over, but he still wasn't stopping by nearly as much as he used to. She would always talk him into coming over, and once he was there, they would have sex. She always waited until after they were done having sex to give Steve an attitude, otherwise he'd get up and leave.

Being locked up at home was not going well for Angelia. She despised the fact that she couldn't leave the house and go after Aliyah. Seeing Steve so happy with her was getting to her as well. Although he stopped by to see her, she knew she wasn't the one making him happy. She started to feel like Steve was doing some kind of charity work by coming to visit her. As she sank deeper and deeper into her anxiety and depression, she thought about aborting the baby at least three times, but didn't have the heart to do it.

Steve had his motel up and running, and was staying busy with the day to day operations. On top of that, he had two new semi trucks with trailers, and his cousins were on the road daily. As his business flourished, so did his relationship with Aliyah. She was teaching him all kinds of new things that he never considered before, and he was able to teach her a few things as well. Aliyah had finally gotten her Maserati back from her ex, and Steve took over the payments and was driving it. He absolutely loved the car. It was fast, powerful, and luxurious. He loved the midnight blue with peanut butter interior, but when he got it, he had it painted white and got very expensive, top of the line rims. The more he drove it, the more he liked it. People were contacting Angelia and telling her how good Steve looked in it. Of course, that made her furious. Steve always had girls chasing after him, but he never paid them much attention. Now that he was driving a Maserati, all the girls were really going crazy. Angelia was on full time house arrest, and she would scroll Facebook and see people talking bout the guys in the city with the nicest cars. Steve's name kept coming up, because his car stood out, and people knew who he was. His car was definitely flashy, but he didn't care since he had such an organized system in place for his cocaine business.

Aliyah started shopping for him, and he began to dress much classier. He always dressed nice before, but he was now out there looking like a fashion model.

The first time Angelia saw him pull up in the car and stepped out in his designer fit, her pussy started dripping. He had never looked so good to her before. When he walked inside, she pulled his pants down and sucked his dick, licked his ass, and fucked him the best she could. Since she was locked up in the house, she tried to keep him controlled with sex. The thing is, that's all he was getting from her. Mentally and emotionally he was clicking with Aliyah, but since they were holding off on the sex thing, he was still getting it from Angelia. She kept him nutting in her pussy and in her mouth. By the time Steve would leave her place, he would be exhausted, completely drained of energy and semen. He would always fall asleep on the phone with Aliyah, and she never really thought too much of it. She just assumed he had been working hard.

Over the next few months, Steve continued to date Aliyah, but he was still stopping by a couple times a week to have sex with Angelia. What Steve was getting from Aliyah was much more than sex, so although he was looking forward to getting with her, they connected on a whole other level, so he didn't mind that she was holding off. One day while he was driving, he noticed that someone seemed to be following him. He wasn't sure if it was someone trying to jack his car or not, so he started to be extra careful. Being followed upset him, and because he had such a good amount of money stacked up in addition to his legit businesses that were bringing in a profit, he considered shutting down his operation. Before he did that though, he wanted to make sure he had a plan to move forward for each and every member of his team. He didn't want to leave anyone hanging.

One day, Aliyah was talking about a crypto coin called Doge coin, and he was planning to get his team together for a meeting to talk about investment opportunities. Angelia had been calling nonstop all day again, but Steve was ignoring her because he was having a date night with Aliyah. Angelia had been hearing rumors from people about seeing the two of them together. She was furious, but there was nothing she could do about it unless she wanted to violate bond. Angelia had started having sex with Ace regularly whenever Steve wasn't around. Every time Ace would stop by, he would give her cocaine, so she pretty much stayed high. This caused her to have even worse emotional problems than she had in the first place. She was spiraling into a dark world of addiction and despair, and all she really felt anymore was anger and the drives for sex and more cocaine. Ace had come to an understanding of what happened between Angelia and Shila, and although Shila's death saddened him and made some challenges with him and the kids, he had forgiven Angelia, truly believing that her intention was never to kill Shila.

CHAPTER
FIFTY-NINE

Angelia sat with her hands folded on the table, listening. "So, you can help yourself out of this situation, Angelia, if you want to. We want to know about Steve, and we are aware that you know what's going on with him. Whatever you don't know, you'd be able to find out without much difficulty. I mean, look at how he's left you right now. You are knocked up, and probably have no money. He put you out of the house, so you are forced to stay with your parents at almost 30 years old. While you sit at home and worry, he's out with his new girl, all lovey dovey. Just take a look at them and tell us what you think." He pulled out several pictures of Steve and Aliyah out at various places. He had pictures of them holding hands and kissing. All of this enraged Angelia because she had been asking Steve regularly if things had been getting serious with Aliyah, but he steadily denied that they were in any kind of serious relationship. What was placed in front of her was showing otherwise. Angelia got red in the face, and she could feel her blood start to boil. "You know, they actually look pretty cute together," the detective said, smiling.

"I bet they'd have a cute baby. I wonder what it would look like?" the female detective added, holding up one of the pictures.

Angelia slammed her hands on the table. "Look! Y'all don't have to rub it in my face! I'm the one that came to you. It was my idea to come and talk to you to see if we could work something out," she said, trying to calm herself back down.

"We are all ears. Go ahead and tell us what you know then," the male detective said, taking a seat across from her.

Angelia looked at them for a moment before saying, "No. First, I want to know what will happen if I give you guys information."

"A lot of things could happen. Really it all depends on you. It depends on what kind of information you give us. We know that you are obviously well aware of everything he has going on. Now, are you going to tell us what you know, or are you going to drip feed us like hamsters, giving us a little here and a little there, but really holding back. That's all on you."

"I told you drugs. What will that do?"

"How much drugs are we talking about here? Does he use them or sell them? An eight ball here and there, or what? Is he selling to a couple buddies just to do it for free himself, or is he actually out there moving product? How much does he have access to?"

"Okay, okay. I get it. I'm just trying to help myself out. What if I called him and asked for 10 kilos of cocaine?"

"Called who? Your baby daddy?"

"Yeah."

"Oh, so he's a drug dealer?"

"I mean . . . yeah. Well, he can get it."

The detectives glanced at each other. The female detective wrote something down on her pad of paper then said, "If we can indict him on ten kilos of cocaine, we may be able to get you 5 years in prison. We would likely be able to get your charge knocked down to manslaughter or something like that. That sure would get you home to your future baby much, much sooner than with the time you are looking at now."

"Damn, that's it? My lawyer said that's what he was going to go for anyway."

"That doesn't mean that he can get it. A lot of lawyers promise a lot of things. What I can do is guarantee you 5 years."

"Can you do better?"

"Can you do better?" the male agent spat back.

Angelia started thinking and sat there silently for a minute. She thought about Ace too, but knew that he mainly moved heroin.

"What about a guy that sells heroin?"

"How much can you get from him?"

"Maybe half a kilo. Oh, wait! He has meth too. What about meth?"

The agents looked at each other and nodded. "How much?" the female detective asked.

"Meth . . . I can probably get 5 pounds of that from him without a problem."

"Okay, let me see here," the detective said as she started writing notes down on her paper again. "You have one guy you can get with 10 kilos of cocaine. You have another guy you can get with 5 pounds of meth and a half kilo of heroin." She paused as she looked at her notes. "If you can make that 6 pounds, you don't have to worry about the heroin. So with 6 pounds of meth, you'd be looking at about three years. And, to be honest, that's probably the best you're going to get out of me, sister."

"Unless you know about a murder," the other agent added, rubbing his hands together and raising his eyebrows.

Angelia replied, "No murders, sorry. I can't help you there."

They put together a plan with Angelia, and she went home. When she got back to the house, she started blowing up Steve's phone again, as usual, to try to get him to stay the night with her. He wasn't responding, and when he eventually did respond, he just told her that he was busy and would have to get with her later. She was pissed off, because he would only come and see her when he felt like it. She was getting tired of begging him to come see her, but that didn't stop her from doing it. Over the next week, Angelia got off her tether. They felt confident that they would have two huge busts with her help.

CHAPTER **SIXTY**

Steve and Aliyah had been in Las Vegas since Thursday evening. It was now late Friday afternoon, and they had a hotel booked for the weekend. Steve was finally letting loose and having a blast. They had just finished a delicious dinner at a world renowned steak house. Steve was able to leave his worries back in Michigan, and was just focused on Aliyah. She, of course, was loving having his undivided attention. Angelia had been calling all weekend, but he didn't answer or respond to her at all. Eventually, just to get her to stop, he sent her a text letting her know that he would call her when he got back into town. He had been walking the strip with Aliyah for about an hour now. At about 9 o'clock that evening there were people all over the place.

Steve and Aliyah laughed as they walked around and saw all sorts of different people. There was always so much to do and so much to see on the strip, but they were only there for a short vacation. While the entertainment was nice, both of them were mostly just loving spending unbroken time together. They went to several different bars and casinos. When they came out of a real cool bar that specialized in classic cocktails, it was getting later in the evening, and they were going to head back to their hotel, or at least get closer. Steve looked at her in her sexy outfit, and was so proud to be with her. She had been proven to be a real solid woman for him.

"So, you think you can live in a place like this one day?" he asked.

"Yes, for sure. Vegas is nice. Some people think that it's just a party city, but it is much more than that. I'll have to show you some of the homes in a nearby area. They are so beautiful, and you will love them. We could have one with our own pool and hot tub," she said as she smiled.

"That would be nice. How much does something like that go for around here?"

"Three hundred to four hundred thousand will get you a great house out here. It's really not much, and I'm talking about a big and nice house. I'm talking 4 bedrooms or more. The market is great out here, and you can get a lot of house for your money. Arizona is like that too."

"Have you been to Arizona before?"

"Yes. One thing about me is that I love to travel and see new places. I've seen so many people just stay stuck in a city and have a narrow mindset, because they never get out to see different kinds of people and cultures. I'm a big foodie too, so I love to try all different kinds of foods. I've even went some places just to go to a restaurant I've heard of. I mean, don't get me wrong, I wanted to go there too, but it was really the food that sealed the deal for me."

"How far is Arizona from here? Have you ever drove there from here?"

"Yes, I have. It's about 5 hours. It really depends on where you are going. But about 4 to 5 hours, give or take. You want to go?"

Steve smiled and thought about it. "Let's do it. I want to go, but if we do, let's rent something fast."

"Yessss," she said, making a fist. "How about a Corvette? A drop top! The new ones are soooo nice!"

"I'm in. We can go tomorrow. I want to see the Grand Canyon."

"We can do that for sure."

Their plans to go back to the hotel changed, and they ended up walking around for several more hours, talking and checking out all the different venues. They couldn't remember how many different drinks they had. They were walking around and checking out any place that seemed interesting to them. By the end of the night, they had went into 8 different casinos and gambled away $15,000. Steve didn't care to spend the money, and he looked at it like money well spent to have a good time with his girl. She was worth it to him.

When they finally got back to their penthouse suite, they were exhausted. Their room was decorated in a clean, modern style. The whole penthouse was covered in black marble floors and countertops. It had all high end appliances. The penthouse had everything you could want in it, and more. The room overlooked a beautiful city view.

CHAPTER SIXTY-ONE

They stood next to each other and looked out the window at the dark night sky accented by the bright, flashing lights of the strip. Aliyah put her arms around Steve and kissed him on the lips. "I'll admit, I've been to Vegas a few times, but I've never been able to pay for anything like this. This is so beautiful. I'm so happy to be here spending time with you. I really appreciate all of this, Steve."

Steve walked over to the wet bar and poured them both a glass of champagne that he had delivered to the room. He walked back over to the window with the glasses, and they both took a drink then he put his hand on her face and kissed her.

Although they had been dating for a few months, they still hadn't had sex yet. She wasn't standoffish about it, she just wanted to wait for the right time. Steve was very understanding, and it didn't bother him at all. He was willing to continue to work for her love. She was worth it to him, so he was more than willing to wait for her.

"You welcome, sweetheart," Steve said as he looked her in the eyes and took another drink.

"So, Juice was asking if me and you were together."

Steve smiled. "What did you say?"

"I told him, yes we are."

"What did he say?"

"He was shocked, but he said he knew that we would hit it off. He knew we were similar to each other and weren't into playing games. You don't mind that I told him, do you?"

"No, not at all. Everyone has been seeing us, so I knew it was coming eventually. And it's the truth, so it is what it is. You're my girlfriend, and one day, you'll be my wife."

She kissed him. "Aww, my hubby," she said and kissed him again.

Later that evening, they were laying in bed watching a movie. Both of them had switched into shorts and t-shirts. She laid on his chest, and they were still sipping on champagne. Steve's mind was thinking about the cars he had seen following him before he left town. He also thought about how the airport security seemed to be a little over the top with him when he was flying in too, but he remembered that they could be like that with anybody. Still, both of those things were on his mind and starting to bother him. He remembered the DEA stopping him as he got on the plane and specifically asked him how much money he had on him. He was happy that he had only brought $7,000 in cash with him, and had put $30,000 into Aliyah's bank account before he left. The whole situation had him kind of shook even though he knew he didn't have anything on him. All of these little signs had him wanting to get out of the drug game completely, and live a completely above ground life.

"So, what's up with the crypto coin I can invest in? You had mentioned that you would let me know when you came across a solid one. You know, we never pulled the trigger on that Doge coin you spoke about before. For some reason, I was just thinking about that."

She raised up off his chest and gave him a big smile. Steve could tell she was instantly excited and energized. "Oh, my God, Steve. I'm so happy you asked. I was just watching something on Doge coin. I was waiting to see if it was going to get formally backed by something. Some popular coins are backed by certain things that give them a monetary value . . . like some sort of technology, you know. But, if you trust me on this one, I'm pretty sure you can make a lot of money. So, listen . . . Doge coin . . . I've been watching it. The time might just be now. I think it's about to take off."

"So what do I need to do? Is Doge coin backed by something?"

"That's the thing. It's not backed by anything, but I'm sure you've heard of Elon Musk, right? The owner of Tesla. I think that, right now, he's the second richest man in the world next to Jeff Bezos, the owner of Amazon. Elon Musk is going to be number one soon, that's for sure. Anyways, he's been Tweeting about this coin like it's the next big thing. He's even calling himself the "Dogefather". This guy is a multi-billionaire. He already moved the market two cents like overnight. I think you should go in on this one. You have to trust me, though. I have way more information on this coin too. I'm just giving you the basics."

"Well, I trust you. How can I get it? I'ma turn on some of my homeboys to it too. How much you think it can go to?"

"I don't know, but even if it goes to fifteen cents, you're going to be making real good money. I'm thinking it might end up closer to fifty cents though, which would be crazy, because it's only 2 cents a share right now."

"Say less. I'ma get my team together when we get back to Michigan. I'ma make all them go in on this."

"See that's what I like so much. I feel like you really trust me and believe in the things I talk about. Everybody else just thinks I'm some kind of nerd or whatever. It's nice to have someone take me serious, and even act on my advice."

"Of course, I believe you. You my little cute nerd. They better stay back," he said, jokingly shaking his fist.

She giggled. "Awww!" She kissed him a few times on his lips. "Your lips are always so soft! They feel like pillows."

"This is how they supposed to be. You can lay right on them whenever you like."

She smiled. "Oh, really?"

CHAPTER
SIXTY-TWO

"Yep," he said, kissing her again and again. She kissed him softly and he moved his hands down her back to her booty. He rubbed her soft booty and massaged it. His hand slid to the bottom of her shorts, and he put his hand underneath them, rubbing her outer thigh. She began to kiss him more passionately, and his hand traveled to the elastic waistband on her shorts. He gently put his finger under the band and started to slide the shorts down. "You trying to lay on these lips?" he whispered.

"I guess," she replied, then went back to kissing him. He kissed her neck and slowly removed her shirt followed by her shorts. His mouth traveled down to her titties, and he began to suck on them while he laid on his back. He put his hands on her hips and moved her up, kissing her stomach, making his way down to the upper edge of her panties. He kissed her panties, and she brought her knees together, and he removed her panties. She got into position, and soon enough, she had her pussy on his lips. It smelled fresh and sweet, almost like strawberry body wash. He kissed around the outside of her pussy and thighs before licking in between her lips then sticking his tongue fully inside her to get a full taste of her.

"You taste so good," he whispered to her.

"I know, baby. You like it?" she moaned as she felt him flicking her clit with his tongue. He alternated between sucking and licking, from gentle to firm, and it was driving her crazy. She was loving how he made her feel, and her whole body was tensing up. It almost felt too good. "Yes, baby. Just like that. Don't stop."

She moved her hips around as he licked and slurped her juices. His whole face was getting wet, as he had his hand on both of her ass cheeks, massaging her to the same rhythm as his tongue. "Oh, shit," she moaned as her whole body got tight, about to cum. He didn't stop, and seconds later, fluids poured out of her as she exploded and shook uncontrollably. "Oh, my God. Hold on," she said as she climbed off his face. "Woah, that's too much for me. I can't take it. I'm sorry," she said, giggling and turning red in the face.

"Come here, baby. You taste good."

Aliyah laid on her back out of breath, and Steve climbed between her legs. He brought his face up by hers and said, "Taste it," as he gave her a long tongue kiss. "It tastes good, don't it?"

"Mmm hm," she said with a somewhat nervous look on her face. "You about to lick it again?"

"I was. You don't want me to? I can be gentle."

"Okay, but be gentle please."

He spread her legs and started licking her clit very softly and barely nibbling on it. She loved it as she laid back and massaged her own breasts. Every time she moaned, it was low and quiet. She wasn't a loud person at all. He pushed her legs back a little further, and made his way lower to see how she felt about her asshole being licked. She didn't jump, pull back, or show any resistance, so he licked her asshole. It was fresh tasting, just like her pussy. He licked around it, slowly playing, and then dug his tongue inside it. She was wiggling around and moaning, but was still very quiet. He kept going, and knew she was enjoying it, then he made his way back up to her pussy. He started licking while he stuck his index finger inside her gently, and began to move it around slowly. Her body responded immediately, and he could feel her getting wetter. Her pussy gripped and released his finger as he moved it slowly in and out. She felt very tight to him. Not too long after, she was cumming again.

"Whooooo, okay! Steve, you proved your point," she said, giggling.

"What point? This is normal," he said, gently kissing her pussy over and over again.

"Give me some of that," she said, as she pointed down below at his dick bulging through his shorts.

Steve was so happy to hear her say that, he didn't know what to do. He had waited a long time for her. His dick was as hard as a rock, and it was throbbing, ready to make its way inside her. He only pulled his shorts down halfway, because he didn't want to wait any longer to be inside her.

"Be gentle though," she said, noticing that he was larger than what she was used to and remembering that it had been a while since she'd done this.

He rubbed his dick between her lips as he held himself over her. He gently pushed the tip between her lips, but felt the resistance. She was definitely tight. He put it in a little, then pulled back out, and did this a few times as gently as he could. He then put the whole tip in, and she pressed her hands against his chest. "Wait, wait, wait. I'm not used to all this. Go slow, please. It kinda hurts."

"Okay, baby. I got you," he said as he began working his dick slowly, barely inside of her. He got about halfway inside of her, then she pushed his chest again.

"Just right there," she said, letting him know where her limit was. He gently stroked her with about half of his dick.

"This pussy is tight, baby," he said, kissing her on her lips. They kissed passionately, and he slid a little more of his length inside her.

"Ohhh! Okay! Hold on. Back up, sir. Too much. Way too much."

"Okay, okay, sorry," he said, pulling out a little. Her pussy was wet, but really tight. He had to really watch himself so he didn't hurt her. He didn't enjoy not being able to let loose on her, but he was so happy to finally be inside her. He tried to push in a little bit more, and she slapped his chest.

"Ouch, baby!"

"Okay, okay," he said, leaving it in and trying to massage around her walls so it felt better. He was now deep enough to make it very pleasurable for him, even though he had to be careful. He stroked her very gently then said, "I'm about to cum, baby. I'm about to cum . . . arggghhhh!" he whispered into her ear as he came inside her. He pushed his dick deeper inside her as he exploded, and she gripped his back with her nails, making him bleed.

"Baby! Damn!" she shouted, feeling the whole length of him pulsing inside her.

"You got it, baby. You got all of it," he said as he let his dick drip inside her until it was empty.

CHAPTER SIXTY-THREE

Steve and Aliyah had been back from their vacation for a few days now. They had explored Vegas and Arizona and had a blast. After their first sexual encounter, they had been having sex every other day, since Aliyah would get sore and was still trying to get used to Steve's size. Steve was patient with her, and actually enjoyed that they were working together to make sure they were both comfortable.

As Steve got back into the normal groove of life, he started feeling funny again about being followed. He was concerned that he was being watched, so he called his team together for a meeting at the MGM Casino in Detroit. His people flew in from different states, and he had rooms set up for them in the casino for two days. There were about 12 of them in total. After they all arrived at the casino, Steve called them together in one of the rooms, and he explained his concerns to them. He told them that it would be best for them all to take a break, because he knew the Feds were on him for sure, and could possibly be on them as well. He didn't know why he was being followed so he wanted them all to be cautious. Steve had a few hundred bricks left in his possession, and he stated that after these ones were gone, they were going to take a break. A few of the guys felt like he was being a little paranoid, but some of the others supported him wholeheartedly, letting him know that it's better to be safe than sorry. Nobody was trying to go to prison.

Steve then moved onto his next topic of discussion, crypto currency. He gave them all a chance to put up $50,000 each into Doge coin. When he brought up the topic, they all started laughing. Everyone thought he was joking, until they saw that he was dead serious, and had data to back up the legitimacy of the investment. He told them that this was a way to an easy million dollars for anyone that was interested. Doge coin was at 2 cents a share. By them investing $50,000, each of them would have 2.5 million shares. After explaining some of the risks to them, along with the strong likelihood that the coin was going to take off, they all agreed to invest. They trusted that Steve wouldn't steer them wrong. Although he was putting his trust in Aliyah, he was fully confident that her research was accurate. He assured them that you only lose if you pull out when the market is down.

Angelia had been blowing up his phone, as usual, and every once in awhile he would answer for her. She had been begging him to come over and have sex with her, but he refused to go see her ever since he started having sex with Aliyah. She knew that he obviously had another source for sex, and that pissed her off, but she tried as hard as she could to not let it show.

Steve had been faithful to Aliyah, and things were going smoothly for him.

Steve awoke from a deep sleep and looked at the time. It was 9 o'clock in the morning. He had a couple missed calls from Angelia, and she had texted him once. He looked at Aliyah, who was sleeping peacefully next to him, then he looked at his phone.

Angelia: Good morning. Are you up?

Steve: Yes, what's up?

Angelia: Why didn't you call me back yesterday.

Steve: I was ripping and running like crazy, my bad. How are you doing?

Angelia: Horrible. I have morning sickness like crazy.

Steve: Damn. You need anything?

Angelia: I told you what I needed. I been telling you for months. You just don't mess with me at all anymore, huh?

Steve: I'm dating someone else. You know that.

Angelia: That bitch.

Steve: Come on now. You ain't gotta be like that.

Angelia: Fuck you. Fuck both of y'all.

Steve: Why every single time I start texting you, we arguing? You don't give me much incentive to respond to you. When you gone cut this shit out?

Angelia: I'll cut it out when you come fuck me.

Steve: I told you I can't do that.

Angelia: Really, Steve?

Steve: Really.

Angelia: So would you be mad if I fucked someone else? I'm horny.

Steve: Lol. I'm sure you already been doing that. I ain't hit that in forever, and I know you ain't waiting around.

Angelia: So you want another nigga nutting all on your baby inside me?

Steve: Damn, you really gone fuck a nigga raw and let him cum inside you?

Angelia: Yeah, if you don't.

Steve: Wow, really Angelia?

Angelia: It's been too long. You need to come over and fuck me. Now.

Steve: You crazy.

Angelia: I can meet you somewhere closer to you. We can do it in the car if you want.

Steve: No.

Angelia: Please.

Steve: No.

Angelia: Can I just suck your dick?

Steve: No.

CHAPTER
SIXTY-FOUR

Steve tossed his phone next to him on the bed. He was tired of playing her games. His phone buzzed. She started sending him pictures of her pussy and videos of her playing with it. Aliyah was still sleeping next to him, but Steve was starting to get irritated with the thought of another man fucking Angelia while she was pregnant. She had done some shit in the past, but he never thought she would be doing that kind of nonsense.

Angelia: Do you miss it?

Steve: I don't want to talk about that. Just stop.

Angelia: Okay, no problem. I'll just go fuck someone else.

Steve: Wow!

Angelia: Come over and get it then.

Steve: I can't.

Angelia: That bitch got you on lock I see.

Steve: No, I got me on lock.

Angelia: That's cool. My dad been asking about you.

Steve: What he say?

Angelia: He wanted you to come through for him like before.

Steve: How many.

Angelia: 10.

Steve: Okay, when?

Angelia: Whenever you can.

Steve: Give me like an hour, and I'll come through.

Angelia: Okay.

Steve got up and got in the shower. After he got out, he brushed his teeth and got dressed. He walked back over to the bed, and Aliyah was still sound asleep. He bent over and gave her a kiss on the cheek.

The sun shined into the garage as the door opened. It was a beautiful morning. Steve got in his Maserati, and glanced at himself in the rearview mirror before backing out. He was feeling himself today. He turned up the radio, and drove off to run a few errands. He stopped to see a couple people. All in all, he was in a good mood. His mom's house was completely paid off, the motel was staying booked and running problem free. The trucks were running well and his cousins were enjoying the work. Steve loved that his choices were making life good for those around him now. He felt like things were finally paying off.

James had continued to upgrade his grow system, so he wouldn't have to spend so much time watering. Although he enjoyed working with the plants, he didn't feel that it was necessary to hand water everything when he could set up reservoirs to feed all of his plants automatically at predetermined intervals.

Steve was in such a good mood, he felt like doing something nice for Angelia, so he stopped at one of their favorite restaurants to get her some breakfast. He wanted to put a smile on her face. He already knew he was going to have to deal with some of her attitude, since he hadn't been by in a while, and she had heard all kinds of stories about him and Aliyah. Aliyah was a Snapchat queen, so she had everybody talking about her all the time and mentioning how cute of a couple they were. When Steve was about three minutes away from Angelia's house, he called her.

"Hello," she answered.

"I'm on your street now. I'm about to pull up."

"Okay. Sounds good. I'll meet you at the door."

"Hey, don't be playing and shit, trying to be nasty when I get there. I know your little slick ass ways."

"What are you talking about? I'd never think of trying anything like that."

"I'm sure you're wearing them little ass shorts, just getting out of the shower conveniently and all that shit."

She giggled. "Whatever, I'm at home. I'm definitely not fully dressed. I do have some sexy stuff on, just to warn you."

"See, that's exactly the type of shit I'm talking about right there. You always on something."

"Byeeee, Steve," she said, and hung up the phone.

Steve laughed and shook his head as he was getting close to her house. Though she had pissed him off, and caused him a lot of problems in the past, he could at least appreciate her attempts to seduce him. She was always good at it, but he had some business to handle today, so he wasn't trying to get caught up in her little games. He decided he was going to stay strong and not give in to her, no matter what.

CHAPTER
SIXTY-FIVE

Soon he arrived, and as he put his car in park and put his hand on the door handle, three unmarked cars and several black trucks pulled in from every direction, blocking him in the driveway, and he froze. Only a few seconds later, police cars came behind them with their lights on. Before Steve could blink his eyes, he saw DEA agents standing on all sides of his car with guns pointed at him.

"Freeze! Get out of the fucking car! Now! And do it slowly!"

"Get your fucking hands up where we can see them!" another one yelled.

"What the fuck?" Steve said as he put his hands up.

Two agents opened the door and yanked him out of the car. They forced him to the ground, and one of them put his knee in his back. They slapped hand cuffs on him while a police officer said, "Haha, we got your ass now!"

"What the fuck is going on?" Steve asked. He was still trying to process how quickly everything was happening.

"Hold tight just a second. We will let you know what's going on." One of the police officers walked him to the back of his police car and opened the door.

"Why are you putting me in the police car?"

"Get in before I make you get in!" the cop yelled. Steve calmly sat in the back to avoid things from escalating. Steve sat there and looked towards the house. Angelia busted out the side door screaming.

She was kicking and screaming as three police officers grabbed her and brought her back into the house. Steve watched as they opened all four doors to his car and started to look inside. They opened the trunk and the hood. By now, there were about 20 unmarked cars that had pulled up. There were Fords, Chryslers, and GMs of all different kinds, and there were all different colored pickup trucks, SUVs, and cars. The whole yard was swarming with agents and officers, and he couldn't even count how many people were there. Before Steve knew it, they were driving off with him. He looked out the window on the way there, glancing back every so often at the trail of cars following them.

When they finally arrived, they pulled Steve out of the back and held his arm, bringing him through a back door. They walked him down a long hallway and put him in a room with gray concrete walls. The only thing in the room was a brown bench.

"In you go," the agent said, pushing him into the room.

"I want to call my lawyer," Steve said.

The agent laughed. "We will let you call when we get ready. You'll get used to doing things when we allow you to do them. Where do you live?"

"I said I want to call my lawyer," Steve repeated calmly.

"I asked where you live, and you didn't give me an answer," the agent spat back.

"You got my ID. Read it."

"Oh, you wanna be a smart ass, huh?"

"You asked me where I live, and I told you. What's going on? Why are you holding me?" Steve asked.

"Investigation. We have a complaint," he said as he slammed the door behind him.

CHAPTER
SIXTY-SIX

The room was completely silent. Steve walked around the room with his handcuffs on for a minute before sitting down. He figured he might be in the room for awhile. He sat there tapping his feet, then eventually stood up and walked around again. He couldn't see anything outside the room. The door was solid steel with a flap that opened from the outside, but it was closed. He looked in the upper corner of the room and saw a camera. Steve paced for a half hour before sitting back down again. His mind wandered off in a million directions, and he couldn't believe that things had finally come to this point. He put his head in his hands and rested until he heard the key go into the door. The door opened and an agent stood there staring at him.

"Where is it?" he asked.

"Where is what?"

"The drugs."

"What drugs? I don't know what you are talking about. I don't know anything about any drugs, and I still need to speak to my lawyer."

"Oh, you want to play games?" The agent laughed, then looked at him with a pissed off face. "We can play games all day. Where were you on your way to earlier today?"

"I was going to my baby momma's house, where you surrounded me at."

"What's her name?"

"Ask her," Steve said, smiling at him.

The agent was not amused. Soon, another agent was standing in the doorway. He looked at Steve for a moment before looking at the other agent. "Nothing," he told him.

"What?" he replied before stepping into the room and approaching Steve.

"What were you dropping off to your baby momma?"

"I was dropping her off 10 boxes of her dad's favorite peanuts and her favorite breakfast. Why? What is this about?"

The agents turned around and walked out, locking the door behind them. That was all they found in his trunk. They had done x-rays on the car and tore the whole thing apart. After it all, they found nothing in the car, except for an owner's manual, breakfast in a to go container, and 10 boxes of Angelia's dad's favorite peanuts.

Although it took a long time for it to sink in, Steve had finally decided to listen to his uncle about trusting Angelia. When she asked him for more coke for her dad, he had a feeling that something was up. He wasn't one hundred percent sure, so he chose to be cautious, and he was definitely glad that he was.

A few hours later, he was released, and went back home to Aliyah. He had James meet him there, and told him the story. James wasn't surprised at all, but he was proud of Steve for not falling for it.

James had a lot of respect for Steve, but he also knew that he had historically made poor choices whenever it came to anything with Angelia. James was so glad that it had finally sunk in for Steve, and that he didn't let her ruin his life.

Two days later, Angelia's bond was revoked. She had been called in for a random drug test, which was part of her bond conditions, and she tested positive for cocaine. When all was said and done, she was sentenced to seven years. Though she tried, she never had a chance to fully set up Ace to get time off her sentence, though she did provide the Feds with information on him.

The prison Angelia was housed at had an email service that all the inmates would use to text their families. Steve had been ignoring Angelia for a while now, since she was always sending crazy emails and talking reckless about things that didn't matter to Steve anymore.

Email from Angelia:

You've been ignoring me since I got to prison and I'm sure you have good reasons. There was a lot I had to get out my system, but now I'm coming to you like a woman. It's been a couple months since you've responded, and I'm getting closer and closer to having our baby. I'm so ready to not be pregnant anymore. Carrying this extra weight around and having this big belly is no fun. Guess what? I just found out what I'm having. I know you wanted a boy, and I did too, but we're going to be the parents of a little girl! I bet she's going to be such a cute baby. Do you think she will look more like me or you? I'm thinking she's going to look just like you. We can work out the names together. I have a few in mind, but let me know what you have first so we can pick one.

So I've been having a lot of time to sit and think and I wanted to say that I'm so sorry for all the things I put you through. At the time everything was going on, I was so caught up in myself that I didn't really have a chance to understand how I was acting. You are such a good man, and I really took you for granted. My cell mate is this older black lady, who is really nice and is full of wisdom. She schooled me on some things and made me open my eyes to a lot of my own flaws and shortcomings. She didn't attack me about them, or come at me sideways or anything. She just asked me a few questions that really got me thinking. This much time in a cell forces you to reflect on a lot of things, so I'm so glad I had her here to guide me, because at first, I was just mad at the whole world.

I was really tripping, chasing the wrong things out there, when I really shoulda been way more supportive of you and what you was building. You were out there looking out for us and our future, making things happen. I was thinking young and looking back, I was so immature. I just wanted to have fun and be seen and you was on something different that I shoulda paid more attention to. I know you not talking to me right now, but I want you to know that I am so sorry for how things played out. If I could go back and change things, I would. I love you so much. Oh yeah, and thank you for the thousand dollars you've been sending consistently every month since I been here. Prison still ain't no fun at all, but having some money in here helps. Oh, and by the way, I'm not going to write you any more crazy baby momma letters anymore. Lol so sorry about that.

Email from Steve:

Hey lady, I was wondering when you was going to write me a normal adult letter. Part of me was starting to think that you wasn't capable of sending one. Yeah, I wasn't trying to respond to all that other stuff. I don't see the point in going back and forth over negative shit while you already in prison. But I'm glad to hear you talking different and doing well now. I'm going to let you chose the name. I trust you on that. I know you will pick a beautiful one that fits our little girl perfect.

Thanks for your apology. It means a lot coming from you, and it shows you've grown since you been in there. The apology is accepted, and I will always love you. And no problem on the money, I have an account set up just for you where it comes out automatically every month on the same date. Let me know if you need anything else.

Email from Angelia:

Wow, I'm glad you wrote back. It's so good to hear from you, but you was so short. You can open up to me. You don't have to be so dry. I want to know what is going on with you. How are you doing? What you been doing? How is the family? I know you hate me for what you think I tried to do to you, but you are assuming things that aren't true. Are you still with Aliyah? The name I think I like the most is Mariah. What you think?

Email from Steve:

I'm not being short, I was just responding. To be honest, I'm really shocked that you wasn't on no bullshit finally. Plus, I was driving at the time and didn't want to get in another accident. I'm doing awesome, so I really can't complain. I just been busy as hell with work. I have like 7 trucks now, and I'm planning to get a few more. The drivers are doing a good job, and the money coming in is great. I have the motel that's doing really well. It's staying pretty full, and everyone is happy that it's fully renovated. I got my hands in a few other things that's going great too. So when you get home, you don't have to worry about anything financially. I'll give you a couple of these trucks plus a nice amount of cash to start your life. I don't hate you at all. Even after everything that went down, I still care about you and want what's best for you. Me and you both know that you tried me, which is crazy, but we going to keep that between me and you. Just please don't mention it to me and try to justify it. Every time you bring it up, it pisses me off, and makes it hard for me to trust other things you tell me. It's over and done with, so just let it be.

My mom been doing well. She's excited that she will be a grandma soon. She helps with dispatching the trucks, and loves it because she can work from home. Yes, I'm still with Aliyah. I'm thinking about proposing to her maybe next year after she has the baby. We still don't know if it's going to be a boy or a girl.

I like the name Mariah a lot. I think it's perfect, and if that's what you like, then go for it. I'm sure she gone be a beautiful little baby.

Email from Angelia:

I'm crying as I type this email to you. Married? Wow, so I guess you really love her? I knew you was dating her, but I didn't think it was that serious. I thought it was supposed to be me and you until the end. What happened to that? I'm happy for you, but this still hurts so bad. Oh my God, it hurts. I guess congrats. I don't really know what to say. Y'all have a baby, plus getting married, damn, I really messed up. You was trying to give me all that, and I destroyed everything… I'm very happy that you growing your business and making your money. Sounds like you are good out there. I will always love you and be here for you when you need me. I'm so so sorry for everything, and I wish I could change how things went down.

My mind wasn't right out there when I was doing drugs. I wasn't thinking properly. I had been doing coke for longer then I told you. You know I was ride or die when it came to me and you, but the drugs really got to me and made me do some real dumb shit. I never wanted to hurt you in any way, and wouldn't have if I was thinking clear, so I'm sorry,

Steve. I'm really sorry and I regret doing what I did. One day, I hope you can forgive me and know how much it hurts me knowing what I did to you. I'm so happy for you with all you have going on, but so sad at the same time. Even though it's hard for me to say, I wish you the best. Maybe one day I will find someone and get married. It's gotta feel nice.

Email from Steve:

Yes, I love her, and I'm in love with her. It was supposed to be me and you, but you messed that all up. I know the drugs was a big problem for you, and you was tripping for sure. Ultimately, you are still responsible for the choices you make though. You made the choices you did, and now you gotta live with them. Hopefully with this time you have, you build yourself up and come back out and be a better woman. I hope you're in there reading good books, and trying to focus on yourself. You still got the same cell mate you was telling me about that was helping you out?

Angelia hadn't emailed back in almost another month. She was hurt and was working on healing herself. Esha and Candy had been visiting her and telling her what was going on in the streets, and that made her want to email Steve again.

Email from Angelia:

Hey, how are you? I miss you so much. Do you think you can come up and see me? That would mean a lot to me. I know you in a relationship but you don't have to tell her, and I'm not going to say anything to no one. I just would like to talk to you face to face about some things. Being able to email is nice, but it's just better to talk about some things in person.

Esha came up and visited me yesterday and told me that you and Juice and a couple others out there looking like millionaires. She wants Juice so bad lol. She told me she seen you driving in a black Lamborghini. Is that your new car? Wow, you are really doing your thing I see. I'm so proud of you. Stay safe and start thinking about me lol Love you.

Email from Steve:

I'm good. How are you? I miss you too, but I don't miss the crazy stuff you used to put me through. It was always something stupid going on. I don't know if I can come up and see you. I just don't feel right about doing that. Of course when the baby is born I will bring her up there to see you often for sure, but I can't come up now.

Juice does not want no Esha lol. She better sit down. That Lambo is Juice's new car not mine. But yes, I got all the guys to invest into that Doge Coin (Crypto Currency) and it made everybody millionaires including me (I just got a couple million). The market went up just like Aliyah predicted, so everyone made a killing. It's the best investment any of us had made. I put up a quarter million into an account for you. That's all you when you come home, and you can do whatever you want with it when you get out. Start thinking about you? lol For what Angelia?

Email from Angelia:

Lmao you are funny. Damn! Y'all made millions off some damn Crypto? (a million is a million!) I don't know nothing about that. And thank you so much! A quarter million? Ayyyeee! I love you! Thank you! And you can start thinking about me. You know you want to. Don't act like you don't remember the love we used to make, and don't act like you don't miss this pussy. You used to be addicted to it. You couldn't stay away. You better know, that will always be my dick forever!!!

READERS DISCUSSION QUESTIONS

1. How do you feel about the videos Steve received?
2. What's your thoughts on Angelia going up to the jail?
3. Were you surprised when Angelia caught Steve and Shila together?
4. Do you think Shila would have been a good girlfriend?
5. Was the investments that Steve made a good idea?
6. What was your response when Angelia was angry about Steve going to the funeral?
7. What's your thought's about Aliyah?
8. Do you know anyone like Steve?
9. What's your thought's about how Angelia did Steve at the end?
10. Should Steve be still trying to help Angelia out?

MORE BOOKS BY A. ROY MILLIGAN

Women Lie Men Lie

Women Lie Men Lie Part 2

Women Lie Men Lie Part 3

Stack Before You Splurge

Naive to the Streets

Girls Fall Like Dominoes

Coming soon

Teen Madam

Self Help books

From Prison to the Car Hauling Game

From Prison to the Publishing Game

Please, please please, leave a review.

https://www.amazon.com/A-Roy-Milligan/e/B009YEVZPC?ref=sr_ntt_srch_lnk_2&qid=1587560927&sr=8-2

Made in the USA
Monee, IL
20 December 2024